From unreality, lead me to Reality.

From darkness, lead me to Light.

From death, lead me to Deathlessness.

Om Peace, Peace, Peace.

- The Upanishads

Monahdah

By

S. J. Zercher

This book is dedicated to my husband, Sunny, and my

daughters, Kailey and Hanna. Thank you for all

the help and encouragement.

There were men of great strength and size on the earth in those days; and after that, when the sons of God had connection with the daughters of men, they gave birth to children: these were the great men of old days, the men of great name. —Genesis 6:4

Anah

The fire is finally hot, and I remove my blanket. Our old, adobe house has baseboard heaters, but Mom doesn't turn them on unless she has to in order to save money. The wood-burning stove inserted into the kiva fireplace does a good job. Even after the fire dies down the adobe walls radiate the warmth of the fire. The glow flickers around the room and onto the pages of the book I'm reading, *The Hobbit*. It's Mom's old copy that she found while organizing the garage.

"Don't you think you need to do your homework, Anah?" She's eyeing me from the other side of the couch, peeking over her romance novel. She's at a juicy part and wants me to leave the room. She's not concerned about my homework and has no reason to be. Her embarrassment is ridiculous, especially since I'm seventeen, practically an adult. Of course, she's right. I should get to my homework, but I'm procrastinating. Homework is so boring.

"I'm almost finished my chapter."

I get a text from Sophia. "What u get for #9?"

"I didn't start yet."

Mom looks over her book again. "Do you have to text right now?"

"It's on silent." I debate whether to leave the warmth of the fire or go to my cold room away from my mother's surveillance and her choice of reading material.

My cell phone buzzes again. Mom's big blue eyes glance over her book. "Anah, do I need to confiscate your phone?"

"It's Sophia with a homework question." This time it's actually Tim asking me again what I'm doing this weekend.

She turns the page. "It's distracting."

I shut my book a little too hard. "I'm going to leave you to your book. Sorry for the distraction." I put the blanket on her. "Here, Mom. Enjoy your book."

"I'm sorry. I'm feeling edgy, I guess. You don't have to leave."

"That's okay. I was going to my room anyway."

My mother is younger than most of the other moms at my school. People often ask if we're sisters. She was only eighteen when she had me. She stares into my eyes sometimes in a sad way remembering my father whom I've never met. No pictures of him exist. Apparently he up and left, and she hasn't heard from him since.

Tim impatiently texts again, "hello!? Ru gonna answer??" I turn off my phone and toss it on my bed. Tim was my boyfriend last year in the eleventh grade. He broke up with me because, he said, he was too busy to be in a relationship. Bullshit. I knew he was lying. He was actually interested in Lori, a senior. I never saw them together; it's just a feeling I get. Like when I was in Ms. Thompson's class one day. She was having an affair with Mr. Brunswick, the band teacher. There was no talk or physical evidence. I just knew, and I really don't know how. It was confirmed one afternoon when I caught them in the band room totally going at it like rabbits. I was looking for Avin, the boy I tutor for math, who's usually working on his composition. Hearing a noise in the far back room where Mr. Brunswick stores instruments, I opened the door. They stopped and looked right at me, and I stood frozen. When I left the room, they proceeded as if I was never there. They looked right through me!

Mom calls them, 'my tricks.' That's why she was so uncomfortable with me in the room while she was reading her romance novel. I can listen in, if I want, to what people are thinking. But I haven't done that in a long time.

I finish my calculus homework in a matter of minutes, seventeen and a half to be exact, as I look at the clock on my bedside table. 10:10. Still early. I don't get tired until at least 1:00 am and even then, many times, I don't sleep. It's more like lying in bed with my eyes closed. Out of habit, I check on Mom and find her asleep on the couch. I put the lid back on her sleeping pills, cover her with the blanket and put another log in the wood-stove. I pluck a little pink pill off the couch and replace it in the bottle. I guess I'd rather it be a bottle of spilled pills on the couch than a glass of wine. I wonder briefly if she'll be okay when I go to college. I hate the thought of her being here alone without me. She'll have to adjust just like I will.

When I set the pill bottle on the coffee table I notice a small notebook open to a list of consecutive numbers written down. All the numbers have been crossed out except for the last two, 179 and 180. I look at her curiously as she lies asleep on the couch.

I Wanted to Fit In

I park in the school parking lot ten minutes late, which means I have to go to the office and sign in. The faculty treats us like infants. I can hardly wait to get out of here and go to college.

I stayed awake until 3am finishing *The Hobbit.* I'm envious of the world Bilbo lives in, full of creatures that were once a part of earth with dragons and real adventure. My life suddenly seems extremely boring. I guess I could have gone to college this year since I was accepted early at Stanford, but I wasn't ready to leave Mom. I'm all she really has.

I enter the classroom for first period, and the teacher is handing out the history exam. A-. I normally get perfect scores, but it drew too much attention. Was I cheating? Was I in the wrong grade? I started to look like some freak. Now I make mistakes to blend in with the other students. The teachers no longer feel uncomfortable or inferior around me. My tenth grade math teacher started to become suspicious of my mistakes, so I learned how to craft better mistakes.

"Pssst…Anah," I hear behind me. It's Tim. I don't want to cause a scene by ignoring him, so I turn around.

"Forgot to charge your phone again last night?"

"No, I forgot how to text," I say sarcastically.

"There's a cool band playing at The Club. Wanna go?"

"It depends," I say with reservation.

"On?" He uses his pencil to scratch his head.

Going out might be good for a change. "Okay. I'll go. But only as friends! In fact, don't come get me. I'll meet you there."

"Yeah, yeah, it's cool. Tonight…7 o'clock."

"Can I bring Sophia?"

"Okay, sure," he says as the bell rings, and we file out of the classroom into the flooded hallway with students.

I'm waiting for Sophia in the hall at the usual spot before we go to calc. She's an attractive brunette with blue eyes. Her dad left when she was only two. Something we have in common.

"Hey!" she says with her beaming smile. "Tim was totally asking about you this morning."

"Yeah, I talked to him already. Which reminds me, do you wanna go see this band tonight?"

"Yeah! Electronic Gypsy's playing. I was going to ask you, actually."

"Tim will meet us there."

Sophia gives me a reluctant look. "I don't want to be a third wheel."

"You won't be. Trust me! We're just meeting up as friends. I'm tired of moping around the house while my mom reads romance novels."

"I'm tired of it too." She links her arm through mine. "You need to get out more, but do you think she'll even let you go?"

"My mom doesn't like me out late, but I'm sure I can get her permission. Don't worry about that."

Sophia smiles satisfyingly. "Cool. I guess I'll go."

Collided

I'm looking for something cool to wear, but I'm not sure how to dress for a psychedelic gypsy concert. My phone buzzes. Sophia has sent me a picture of what she's wearing. I rummage through Mom's closet. She's at the Roadrunner where she works, a small local restaurant right off the interstate. I'm relieved she didn't give me any problems about my plans.

Man, she has a lot of clothes that I've never seen before, like this suede vest with red silk on the back. This black dress could work…or this cool leather jacket. I'll wear it with jeans since it's too cold out for a dress. I top it off with some boots, check myself out in Mom's wardrobe mirror and tie my hair up into a messy bun. Not too bad.

Something tells me that Mom is getting ready to call, so I look at my phone in anticipation. My phone buzzes.

"Hi, Mom."

"Did you leave already?"

"Not yet. Why?"

There's a long pause, and I know what she's about to say. My blood boils.

"I don't think you should go out tonight."

"Mom." I take a deep breath, "It's totally fine. I'm going to be with Sophia and Tim. I'll be back before you're even done at work."

"Okay, but don't talk to any strangers."

"Really? Mom, I'm not a child. It's perfectly fine and safe."

"Nothing's perfectly safe, Anah."

"Please, Mom, don't worry so much. I'm going to be in college soon, you know. You're gonna have to get used to my independence."

There's silence on the other end of the phone. She can't win this battle. Not this time.

I bite my tongue. "Okay then. See you soon." I hang up disappointed that we had to have that conversation again. She's gotten a little better about me going out with my friends, but she's always been overly protective of me. If she had someone other than me in her life maybe she wouldn't worry so much. She doesn't want me to end up like she did,— a young, pregnant teenager. Her parents died in a car accident a few years before she had me. They were hit by a drunk driver. Her mom's best friend took her in. She was a senior in high school when she dropped out and got a job. When I was two, she found a sitter so she could work nights. Her name was Miss Bee. She smelled like mothballs and weighed two hundred pounds. When I heard her thoughts, she was cynical and negative and very jealous of Mom because of her beauty. I would pretend to be asleep in my crib and anxiously wait for my mother to safely return home. She would kiss me goodnight and say, 'I love you, Anah.' She was sad, and I was the only thing that kept her going.

The Club's big parking lot is full, so I have to park down the street. The line of people waiting to get in stretches around to the back of the building.

My phone buzzes in my back pocket with a text from Tim. "Hey where ru?"

"jus got in line"

"Meet us at door. Have tix"

I find them easily, and Sophia and I hug the way we normally do. Tim hands me a ticket. "Thanks, Tim. How much do I owe you?" I smirk. "Remember this isn't supposed to be a date."

"I know. Don't worry about it. My dad got me the tickets."

"Oh, that's right. I forgot your Dad's the manager of the radio station. Don't let me forget to thank him."

"You look great, by the way," he says as his cheeks redden.

"Thanks." I smile enjoying a little attention, but I tell myself to keep my emotions secure.

Sophia whispers in my ear, "I knew I was gonna be a third wheel."

I don't have a chance to respond to her because Tim's dad introduces the band over a loud speaker, and the audience claps and cheers. The band members look theatrical, like they're about to perform a play, wearing top hats, and suspenders with pinstripe pants. I like what the girl wears, a short black frilly skirt with black mesh tights and combat boots.

I stick my hands into the pockets of the leather jacket and feel something in there. I pull out a ring. Mom must have left it in there and forgot about it. I slide it down my index finger. It's amazing! The silver metal coils around three times with a lava red stone that actually seems to glow. I'm unable to make out the intricacies, so I decide to go to the bathroom where there's more light.

"I'll be right back," I say loudly into Sophia's ear so she can hear me over the music.

She and Tim are really enjoying themselves, dancing and singing. They obviously know the songs. She nods her head in response.

I push my way through the dancing crowd toward the bathroom, looking down at this little piece of treasure I've found. As I turn the corner to the bathroom I bang into a very large guy. I look up and freeze. My heart trembles. He's gorgeous. He wears a thin, black, well-fitted sweater.

"Excuse me." His deep voice makes me blush. He looks down at the ring on my hand. The orange and red glow of the stone reflects in his eyes.

I feel tongue tied. "…..Uh… sorry."

He places his hand on my arm and there's a tingling sensation. "I should be less reckless."

I wait for him to go around, and I open the door to the girl's bathroom. That was a little weird.

I look down at my finger. It's a little big but too cool for words. I can't decide what the stone is since I've never seen anything like it.

"Holy shit," I say out loud. The ring moves and wraps around my finger into a perfect fit. It happened so subtly that perhaps I imagined it. I brush it off. Now I'm seeing things.

I decide to use the facilities while I'm in here. There are oddly two sets of feet in the stall next to me. A pair belongs to a girl, who is strangely wearing the same boots as me, and the other pair belongs to a boy. God knows what goes on in these bathrooms.

My thoughts wander back to the guy I just bumped into. I take the keys out of my back pocket and place them on the hook on the door to avoid dropping them into the toilet. I'm captivated by this stranger and realize I'm wearing a smile on my face. A delicious scent of him lingers over me, and I want to go back out and nonchalantly look for him.

I wash my hands and give myself a quick look over in the mirror before I return to the venue room. The crowd is singing along, or I should say hissing along making it sound like we're in a room full of snakes. The band encourages the audience to interact, instructing us to hiss as they sing, creating an interplay of sounds.

I rejoin Sophia and Tim, and they are really into it. I glance around the room looking for my mystery man when our eyes meet. He was already looking at me. My heart thumps an extra beat. Suddenly feeling strange, I look down at my finger to see the ring glow bright orange and red.

"Are you all right?" Sophia yells into my ear, breaking me out of my spell.

"Yeah, the band's really cool. I'm gonna go sit down for a minute."

I ask for water at the bar and look around but don't see him anymore. This ring is glowing so bright I wonder if I should put it back in the pocket.

"A gift from your boyfriend?" I hear the familiar deep voice behind me. It's him!

"W-what?" I stammer. "I mean, give me what?" He's referring to the ring, of course.

"You keep looking at that ring."

"Right, I ah… found it."

His eyes narrow, and he scoffs.

"What's so funny?"

Our eyes lock. Time stands still, and you would never know we were in a loud room full of people dancing and singing. I didn't want to disturb these few seconds of magic, and perhaps I stare too long.

His lips are ruby red, and his eyes — a pale aqua marine that captures light like the ocean. His scent is intoxicatingly sweet with a hint of cinnamon. His hair is well kept, short and slightly coarse and is a strange combination of blond and brown giving it a beautiful caramel color. It dawns on me that he hadn't been yelling into my ear. He was talking as if we were in a quiet room, yet I could hear every word perfectly.

"You seem so enamored by it."

"Yeah... well, I just found it."

"Maybe it belongs to someone here, and they dropped it."

"Right into my pocket." I smile at the implausibility. "Actually it's my mother's leather jacket."

"You should ask her about it when you get home."

"I'm curious about the stone." I rest my arm on the bar as I become more relaxed talking to him. "I have no idea what it is. Do you know anything about gemstones?"

"Let me see." He touches my hand. A tingling sensation travels up my arm. I can feel his warm breath on my skin when he bends down to look. If it were quiet, he would hear my heart pounding out of my chest. Oddly, the ring glows even brighter. His eyes shift to look at mine. "It's definitely one of a kind."

The song ends, and everyone claps and cheers. "I would like to see you again," he says while he looks at the band and claps.

"Shouldn't you at least ask me what my name is first?"

He turns and looks at me quizzically. "I'm sorry?"

My face reddens! I thought for sure he said something. This pause is extremely awkward! "Sorry, I thought you said something."

"I'm Victor." He puts his hand out.

"Anah." Our hands clasp.

There's something strange and very different about Victor. He seems out of place, but somehow, on a mysterious level, I can connect with him.

Sophia marches over in our direction. "Anah, where the hell've you been?" She eyes Victor.

"Oh...Sophia, sorry. I'm coming." I rejoin Sophia and glance back. I could have sworn he said something again, but he wasn't speaking at all. "Bye, Victor, nice meeting you."

He smiles back at me, and I feel warm all over. My face must be beet red. I've never experienced an immediate attraction to a stranger before. I know it sounds ridiculous, but it's like I have to be near him.

Forget Something

It's 10:15. Oh darn, I'm going to be late. I give Mom a quick call, before she panics, to let her know I'm on my way and everything's fine.

People linger in small groups outside in the parking lot, passing out cigarettes and lighting up. "Ok, the suspense is killing me, Anah." Sophia lights up a cigarette she has bummed off someone. "Who was that guy?"

"I've never seen him before." Tim takes the cigarette from Sophia and takes a hit.

"I collided with him on the way to the bathroom. His name's Victor."

Sophia exhales. "He seemed really into you."

I decide to change the subject. "Look at the ring I found in my mom's jacket."

Sophia looks with amazement. "How does it glow like that?"

"I'm gonna ask her about it when I get home. It's odd that she has it in this jacket that I've never seen her wear, and she doesn't even wear jewelry."

"Maybe she'll let you have it."

"Thanks for the ticket, Tim. It was really cool." This whole magical evening wouldn't have happened otherwise.

"Yeah, Tim, I never realized what a cool guy you are."
Sophia smiles her signature smile and gives him a hug. Their hug
gives me that weird yet familiar, intuitive feeling, and I know
they're going to hook up.

I leave the cloud of smoke, and head in the direction
of my car. "Call me."

Sophia waves. "As soon as I get home."

I have to walk a ways to reach my car, so I get my
keys out well in advance. A streetlight goes out while I search
around in my pant pockets and the pockets of the leather jacket.
"Shit!" I try to remain calm, but panic starts to kick in as I fumble
around in the dark. I race over in my mind what I did with them.
The bathroom! Damn! I was so caught up in the moment I left
them hanging on the hook behind the bathroom door. I turn to
run back, but Victor stands right behind me. The street light
flickers back on. "Forget something?" He holds out my car keys.

This is really weird...I mean, how the hell did he
know they belonged to me? I try not to appear frazzled. "Oh, gee...
thanks Victor."

"They were asking everyone on the way out if
anyone lost keys."

"And you knew they belonged to me?"

"They didn't belong to anyone else who was still
inside, so I did the math."

"Oh. Then I really appreciate you doing your math," I joke.

"It's cold and late. You should get back before your mother worries. I'll escort you to your car."

Despite the attraction, I feel uneasy since Mom has drilled into me to never talk to strangers, and I know he can tell. He stares at me briefly, and I suddenly feel more relaxed. I send Sophia a text as a safeguard. "Call me and make sure I arrive home ok. With Victor."

He walks me to my car. Can he hear my heart pounding? I unlock the car, and he opens the door for me and says, "My queen."

I narrow my eyes at him. "That's a bit much, don't you think?"

"Your ring. It's very royal." The street light shines bright enough that I can see a hint of a smile.

My body feels so energized since I put it on. I look at the ring again, and it's glowing very bright. Is it because it senses my elated mood? Is it Victor's presence? Is it a coincidence that it was glowing this bright during our first encounter? Something tells me I will learn the answers to these questions very soon.

Between Sips

Before I open the door, I decide to take the ring off and slip it back into the pocket of the leather jacket. I'll talk to Mom about it later. I don't want a potential argument to spoil my evening. That way I'll fall asleep in bliss, that is, if falling asleep is an option. I'm still very much awake from the excitement.

Mom is sitting in her robe at the kitchen table with a cup of tea.

"Sorry I'm late, Mom."

"What happened?" She asks rather sweetly, so I don't worry about repercussions.

"Well, the band played till the bitter end, and it was really fun, actually. Tim's dad got us the tickets. Wasn't that sweet?"

"Yes."

I was waiting for a "but," but it never came. This night might end with perfection.

My phone buzzes. "ru home!! Call me!" Sophia texts.

"Yes. Call u later."

"Would you like some tea?" Mom begins to get up. "I just made a pot."

"Sure, I can get it."

"My jacket looks nice on you. Don't forget to put it back."

"I hope you don't mind. You have so many cool clothes you never wear."

"Between here and work, I don't have any reason to wear them."

"When's the last time you wore this jacket?"

"Oh, I don't know. I don't remember... Way back in the—" She stops in mid-sentence.

"What's wrong?"

Slowly she puts her teacup down and looks at me. "Give me the jacket," she says evenly.

"Right now?"

"Yes, take it off, and give it to me, please."

I don't like her tone and hope this isn't where we crash and burn and end the night horribly.

I remove the jacket and hand it to her. She puts her hand in the pocket and pulls out the ring.

"That's probably not the best place for your ring," I say smugly.

"I didn't want to put it with my other jewelry," she mumbles. "It seemed like a good place at the time."

"Where did you get it? Why don't you ever wear it?"

"It was a gift, and it's not for me to wear." She's thinking of someone she has strong feelings for. I tell myself not to pry into her mind, but it's suddenly hard to resist.

"What do you mean? Why not wear it? It's awesome."

"Because," she takes a sip of tea and swallows loud, "it belongs to you." Her eyes begin to swell with tears.

"Why haven't you given it to me?"

"You were to find it when it was time. The right time for you."

I'm not used to her talking mysteriously. It doesn't feel right. "Mom, why all the mystery? Just tell me. It's just a ring."

Sipping her tea, she sighs, and now looks complacent. "You're right. It's just a ring, and it's yours, so you may have it. I'm really tired, Anah." She kisses me. "Goodnight."

"But wait," I protest.

"We can talk about it tomorrow, if you want," she says as she puts her cup into the sink.

"You can at least tell me who it's from."

"If you promise we can talk about it later when I'm not so tired."

I know what she's going to say. I feel it in my chest, and the words rumble into my ears, before she opens her mouth. "The ring is from your father."

3:30 am

I roll over again and give my pillow another punch. It's 3:30 in the morning. I wish I could sleep like a normal person, but I'm too angry now anyway. Thoughts rumble around inside me like a storm. Mom drops a bomb on me like that and then refuses to talk about it! I have so many questions now, and I don't know where to begin. They ping pong around in my head. My father gave me this ring but wanted me to have it when I was ready. Ready for what? Where did he go? Why did he leave us? I want to meet him. That's what! And no excuses this time. Why did he leave in the first place? And why didn't he want me? I have the right to know. I'm angry with myself because I'm crying. Grow up, Anah, you're not a little girl! But I've been saying that my whole life. I never allowed myself to be a little girl. I feel pain in my heart and a lump in my throat. The ping pong ball bounces around some more. I hate him. I miss him. How can you miss someone that you've never met and don't remember? I wonder what he looks like. It's sad to think that if I bumped into him on the street I wouldn't know it. I acknowledge for the first time the empty hole in my heart and the hard outside shell I created to not just fool others but myself.

Something interrupts my thoughts. My body quivers and a prickly sensation covers my cranium. *"Victor?"*

"Yes."

I didn't just hear that! Right? I shrug it off like it was my emotional state of mind. His voice though was as real as the bed I lay in. I can't shake this feeling that Victor and I have an intense connection. I'm sure I heard him speak to me at the concert when he didn't. The origin of this sensation begins deep inside my chest. I used these 'tricks' as a child to hear people's thoughts. It was a very natural ability. The thoughts and feelings people have can be frightening and very unwelcoming to a child. Like with my babysitter's thoughts. When I learned to turn it off it sounded like a mixture of background noise and static. Being alone in nature was a way for me to remedy the noise.

I put myself back in the moment of meeting Victor, replaying every second in my mind, and I realize that he withheld something from me.

Mon

Victor takes off his favorite sweater. He got use to wearing jeans in order to blend in, despite the lack of comfort. His geometric Sri Yantra tattoo covers his upper back.

He's giving himself another chance to find a mate before the ship arrives, and he hasn't had much luck until tonight. Anah would be a perfect mate. He's surprised and baffled by her. She could hear his thoughts, and she didn't seem to realize it. He needs to find out who she is and how she got access to that ring.

He picks up the Mon stone off of his bookshelf and holds the perfect red sphere in his hands — The same kind of stone as Anah's ring. It glows brightly when he picks it up. He closes his eyes and allows the stone's energy to revive him.

He returns the stone to the bookshelf and the fragmented, swirling light comes to a rest.

Eight Hundred Acres

Mom shakes me awake. *What the hell? It's the weekend, isn't it?*

"Anah, you have to drive me to work."

I don't open my eyes. "Why?"

"My car isn't starting."

"Give me some time to wake up," I say yawning.

"I was supposed to be there ten minutes ago."

"Tell them you're gonna be late then."

"You can have breakfast when we get there."

Her bribe works, so I climb out of bed, throw on jeans, my favorite tee shirt and my jean jacket. My eyes are a little red from crying last night, so I throw some hot water on my face. I put my knit hat on because of the cool morning temps but mostly because my messy hair screams for one.

It's too early for conversation, so we drive the ten minutes in silence, although my thoughts weigh heavily on my father. All of my questions will have to wait.

The parking lot is jam packed. "Busy morning," I say.

"You can park there." She says pointing at a spot that says, 'employees only'. "Are you coming in for breakfast?" "Sure," I say yawning.

There's already a line forming, but Mom seats me right away at the counter. I'm looking at the menu, even though I know it by heart, and sense someone staring at me. Whoever it is whispers to the old man between us. The old guy glances over at me and gives me a creepy wink before he moves. My heart skips a beat when Victor takes his place.

"We meet again." He straddles the stool. It looks way too small for him. Mom interrupts. "Good morning, Victor. What can I get for you this morning?" She uses her sweet voice.

"The usual," he says.

I narrow my eyes at her. She said his name! "You know him?"

"Sure. He's a regular." She writes on her pad. "Victor, this is my daughter..."

"Anah," he finishes. "I had the pleasure of making her acquaintance last night at the concert."

"Ok, let me get your orders in right away. Anah, the usual?"

"Yeah, with a side of eggs."

"Two orders of pancakes on the way." She disappears into the kitchen.

I nervously adjust my hat. "I've never seen you here before."

"Neither have I seen you," he says. "Your mother is wonderful," he adds. "She serves people from her heart and never expects anything in return. I bet she takes home the most tips."

"I wouldn't know. She doesn't talk about her tips. She never talks about money actually."

"Precisely what I mean."

"It's funny how we meet for the first time last night, and we're bumping into each other again the next morning."

"And we both ordered pancakes." His caramel lashes blink. "That's just how the universe works."

"You know how the universe works?" I grin sarcastically.

"It doesn't work, it just is."

"You have an accent. Where are you from?"

"We move around a lot, so it's a combination of places." He fiddles with his silverware. "I was hoping I would see you again."

I feel warm all over. I still have my jean jacket on and take it off. Victor helps. "You can thank my mom's piece of shit car for that. Had it started, I wouldn't be here right now." I'm not usually very good at talking to guys, but for some reason Victor makes me feel relaxed. "Do you live nearby?" "Not far. About forty-five minutes from here up on the Glorieta mesa. How did you like that band last night?"

I get the feeling that he's not really into small talk but wants to keep my attention. "I thought they were fun… entertaining. Forty-five minutes isn't exactly close by. You must really like the food here."

He rests his elbow on the table and pivots in my direction on the stool. "I like to be around people."

I notice that our legs are practically touching. "You must live out in the middle of no man's land up there on the mesa."

"We own a lot of property."

"Ranchers?"

"No, but we have horses and goats. We grow our own food."

"How many acres?"

"I actually don't know, but I could easily estimate that it's about eight hundred acres." He looks down at my hand. "Did you ask about the ring?"

Our food comes at the same time. "Bon appétit," says the cook as he quickly drops the plates down.

"Yeah." I look for the syrup, and he passes it to me without me asking. I pour a little over my pancakes. His eyes stare directly into me as if he's searching for something. Why is he so interested in my ring? He pours syrup onto his pancakes.

"And?"

"It's really nothing. My father, who left when I was too young to remember, left it for me. I guess he thought a ring might make up for things." I stab my fork into my eggs and take a bite before I reveal another vulnerable emotion.

"I'm sorry to hear that." He takes a bite of his pancakes without looking away.

My eggs need pepper, and before I say or do anything, Victor passes me the pepper. "Thank you. You read my mind." I force a smile to cover up my uneasiness about how he seems to know what I'm thinking. "I'm gonna talk to her about it later. Maybe I can find out where he lives."

"You have no memory of him?"

"He left when I was a baby so…" In a flash, I have an image of a man holding me, telling me he'll be back and not to worry. "So… how… could I remember?" Victor gives me a curious look. Boy, the mind can easily play tricks on us. That must have been my mind trying to create lost memories and fill in the blanks.

I realize they brought me a side of sausage that I didn't order. "Do you want my sausage?"

"No, thank you. I don't eat meat or consider it food."

"You're a vegetarian?"

"I eat what's food and not eat what's not."

"Sometimes I eat meat, like at Thanksgiving."

My heart beats with anticipation because I know what he's going to ask me next. It's loud as thunder in my chest. "Maybe we can get together sometime. What's your number?"

I tell him my number, but he doesn't write it down. "Do you want me to write that down for you?" I would be able to remember but most people wouldn't. "I'll remember," he says as he taps his finger on his temple. Then he reaches in his pocket and puts money on the little ticket tray. "See you soon."

I try not to stare as he walks away. I thank Mom's car for the luckiest day of my life.

Donny Darko

Why our paths haven't crossed before is strange. Outside of school, there's not too many places to hide in this town. What's really strange is the way he seemed to know what I was thinking. I didn't hear him in my head this time, but he seemed to clearly hear my thoughts.

I check my phone. I have a text from Sophia. "Can I come over?"

"Sure☺" I text back.

"In 15."

I quick pick up my clothes off the floor and make my bed. I'm not a tidy person but Sophia is, and I dislike it when she sees my mess.

There's a knock at the front door. "Come on in, Soph," I yell, knowing it's her. I greet her with a hug and get a whiff of her new habit. "Hey, what's up?"

"Oh… you know, jus got in a fight with my mom."

I lead the way to my bedroom. "Over what?"

"You know. The usual stuff… money, college. I'm applying to colleges out of state, and she told me not to bother because she can't afford to send me to them."

"Maybe you can get a scholarship."

"That's what I told her." She plops herself on my bed. "She's so negative all the time."

"What do you want to do?"

"We don't have to do anything…. jus wanna hang out."

That's what I like about Sophia. She's so easy to please.

"We could make brownies and watch a movie."

She crosses her legs on the edge of the bed. "Awesome."

We round up the ingredients on the kitchen counter. I crack the eggs into the bowl, while Sophia stirs the chocolate mix.

"Guess who was at the Roadrunner this morning?"

"Who?"

"Someone you thought seemed really into me last night at the concert."

"You saw that guy, Victor?" she asks with her excited high-pitch voice that for some reason doesn't bother me.

"Yep. Can you believe it?"

"Did you talk to him?"

"We ate breakfast together. He had to leave suddenly, but he asked for my number."

"He's hot, Anah."

"There's something different about him."

"Like what?"

"I don't know how to explain it. He's just different from anyone I know." I don't want to admit that he seems to know what I'm thinking. I've never told Sophia about my unusual ability to hear peoples thoughts. I promised Mom that I would keep this to myself. Most of the time I think I'm crazy. That's how I rationalize things… by thinking it's only my imagination. "And apparently he's a regular at The Roadrunner. My mom totally knew him and everything."

"I've never seen him around before."

We put the brownies in the oven and look for a movie to stream. We decide to watch Donnie Darko even though we've seen it before.

The timer rings for the brownies, so we pause the movie.

The movie has me thinking about time travel, and I ask her, "If you had one chance to travel anywhere in time, where would you go?"

"I would travel to the past so I could meet my Dad."

"Yeah, me too." The smell of chocolate fills the air. We sink our teeth into the brownies and watch the rest of Donnie Darko.

The Sun Was Black

Weird dreams wake me up. My t-shirt's drenched with perspiration, so I find a new one in my drawer. I try to recollect my dreams, but there were several. They replay in my head out of order, and I try to sort it out. A spaceship landed in a field. People were boarding. I was wearing the ring my father gave me, and it was glowing brightly. I didn't want to board the spacecraft because they wouldn't let Mom on board, but a man who I think was my father let her on. The sun was black, and I was running away from something that was trying to kill me. Then Victor and I were flying through the air, but it felt more like falling into total blackness.

I look out my window and everything's covered in a blanket of white. It snowed! The sun shines bright and not a cloud can be seen. This brings me back to reality, and I forget about my weird dreams. It's not too common, but it can snow in September at higher elevations. It will probably melt by this afternoon.

I hear voices from the kitchen. Mom giggles.

Who is she talking to? The voices are coming from the kitchen. I smell pancakes and realize how hungry I am. I stop at the kitchen and stand dumbfounded. What am I seeing? "Good morning, Anah," Mom says, with a bright face. I'm unable to say anything because my mouth is agape staring at Victor in the kitchen making pancakes. "Victor came by to see you, but you were asleep. I told him he could wait."

"I made some pancakes for breakfast. I guess it's almost lunch now, isn't it?" he corrects himself. Mom laughs.

"Umm, how long have you been waiting?" But before I hear an answer I say, "Um, I'll be right back. I need to…" I make a beeline to the bathroom. I look at myself in the mirror and quickly run the brush through my hair and brush my teeth. How the hell did he know where I lived? His charm is obviously infectious because I've never seen Mom so smitten with any of my boyfriends before. Wait, what am I saying? He's not my boyfriend! I try to collect my nerves and return to the kitchen. I do love pancakes.

I sit down to a plateful of perfectly, cooked pancakes. Mom pours syrup on her pancakes. "Victor was calling you," she says.

"Oh, sorry. My phone probably needs to be charged," I say adding syrup. I come to the realization that Victor is at my house and that we're eating his pancakes.

"I saw how beautiful it was outside and wanted to share it with you," Victor says. I'm embarrassed by how open he is in front of Mom. I glance over at her, and she has a silly grin on her face.

"Victor fixed my car," Mom says before she takes a bite.

"You fixed her car? And pancakes?"

"Anah, I think you're being a little rude. Victor came all the way, on his horse, to see you."

"What?" I bark. "You rode a horse here?"

"Yes, and if it's okay," he looks at Mom, "I would like to take Anah for a ride before the snow melts."

"Is it safe? I mean, with both of you on the same horse?"

"Perfectly. I'll keep at a walk, and we won't go far."

"Excuse me, but shouldn't you ask me first if I want to go?"

"Of course, only if you want to." He raises an eyebrow and smiles. He knows that I totally want to.

"I'll change my clothes and be right back." I'm rushing around my room looking for a pair of comfortable riding jeans. It's been several months since I've been riding, so I hope I don't embarrass myself. I put on a wool sweater that I usually wear skiing, but it's perfect for this in-between kind of weather. I splash hot water on my face and quickly gargle. I don't have time to wash my hair, so I put it back in a braid.

Amanda

He's a beautiful gray. I stand mesmerized by this incredible creature in my yard. Victor slides his hands down each leg, inspecting each hoof. Then he unbuckles the girth and removes the saddle.

"Is everything ok?"

"Everything's fine. I want to go bareback. The saddle takes up a lot of room."

I must look uneasy because he tells me not to worry. "We'll take it slow, and see how it goes."

He gets a leg up from our fence and slides onto the horse's back with ease. He's gorgeous. Victor, this time, mounted on this beautiful stallion. He looks more like a man, and I suddenly feel a little self-conscious.

"*Her* name's Amanda," he says emphasizing *her.*

Mare, that is. They're obviously a team and look like they could ride off into battle. I run my hand along her smooth neck. Her long mane is as white as the snow. "Hi, Amanda." Her long, white lashes blink, and her bright eyes stare into mine.

"I found her in nature," he says.

"In nature? Do you mean in the wild?"

"That's what I mean, but she wasn't wild. I hardly did anything to train her."

"Then how do you know she was wild? You probably found someone else's horse."

"I was the first person to lay hands on her."

"How do you know that?"

"She told me."

I smile at my thought. Victor is odd. He hardly seems like a typical guy, at least not like the ones I know.

Victor reaches out his arm and pulls me aboard. He takes my hand and places it around his waist. I reach around with my other hand. His body is warm, and he smells like sweet cinnamon.

"Hold on to my waist, and you'll be fine." The vibration of his voice comes from my chest and into my ears. Okay...there it happened again! This is the second or third time I thought I heard him talk to me without saying a word. It's faint, but I hear it clearly.

He clucks, and Amanda walks on through the rising mist coming from the piñon and cedar trees as the warm sun melts the layer of snow. Except for the sound of Amanda's breath and the steady rhythm of her gait, it's quiet. We ride in silence for a long time. It isn't awkward but peaceful. Victor enjoys this exactly the way he intended, so I don't want to break the spell. I find myself falling into a deep meditative state until we stop. Victor holds my arm to assist my dismount.Trying to look as graceful as possible, I swing my leg over and slowly slide down Amanda's body. I've never been a clumsy person, and I don't want Victor to see me look otherwise. "Why did we stop?"

"Amanda wants to graze here." She has her muzzle in the snow eating the grass underneath.

He takes my hand again, and we walk hand-in-hand to a boulder at a warm sunny spot. "I'm sorry I showed up at your house today." He smiles from the side of his mouth. "I freaked you out, I think."

"It's okay. It wasn't totally unexpected." I tuck a loose strand of hair behind my ear. "How did you know where I lived?"

"I just asked your mom. I told her I wanted to see you."

"She never mentioned it."

"I wanted it to be a surprise."

My thoughts drifts to my ring and the conversation I haven't had with Mom yet.

He shifts his weight on the rock we're sitting on. "Where's your ring?"

"It's on my bedside table." I narrow my eyes. "It's funny. Sometimes I get the feeling you know exactly what I'm thinking," I finally confess.

"I don't know. I just pay attention. Just like I knew that Amanda wanted to graze here. She couldn't tell me that of course. I pay attention."

"That's how you knew yesterday at breakfast that I wanted the pepper?"

"Sure, and you were looking right at it."

"I could have been looking at the salt."

"Lucky guess." He moistens his lips. "You said yesterday that your father gave it to you."

"Yeah, and my mom said I would find it when I was ready."

"Ready for what?"

"I don't know. I want to talk about it, but she's avoiding the subject. I could manipulate her into..." *Oops.* "I mean, I want her to tell me on her own, when she's ready." I try to hold back the tears swelling up, and I feel that lump in my throat again. "I don't know anything about him."

Victor wraps his arms around me, and I settle into his chest. It feels really nice. The sound of his heart is strong and comforting. There's something about him that makes me feel like I can be myself. It's also very unfamiliar territory since I'm not used to letting myself open up to someone.

"Sorry...this is really unlike me."

"It's okay, you don't need to apologize for me." His face is really close. I look into his eyes and sense a deep longing. Waves of desire flutter to my heart.

"We've been gone long. Perhaps we should head back," he says without looking away.

I shyly look away. My face must be beet red from blushing. "Yeah. The sun is already setting."

He leads Amanda to the boulder, takes a step up and swings his leg over in one easy move. He reaches for my arm, and I climb on board. I'm not shy this time about our bodies touching. "Hold on tight!" Victor says as he instructs Amanda with a whistle. I wrap my arms tightly around his waist, and Amanda opens her gait to a smooth and lovely lope across the meadow.

The ride home is quiet. We both seem to be relishing our time together that questions would only spoil. One question could lead to another, so I decide they can wait. I will get to know him soon enough, I sense, so I'll enjoy the mystery while it lasts.

When we reach my house I smell fresh piñon smoke rising from our chimney. The upper ridge glows orange with the setting sun marking the perfect end to my day with Victor. He leads Amanda into our vacant corral, saddles her again and tightens the girth.

The crackling fire in the wood-stove provides a welcoming warmth when we walk through the door.

"I was beginning to worry," Mom says. "How was your ride?"

"It was wonderful. Thank you for letting me steal your daughter for the day."

Mom looks at me with approval and back to Victor. "Would you like some hot chocolate? Something to warm you up?"

"I wish I could, but it will be dark soon, and I need to get Amanda home."

"Of course," she says. "Thanks again, Victor, for fixing my car."

"I was happy to be of service."

As soon as we go back out he wraps his hand around mine. He stops and turns with his eyes pouring into me. "Would you like to see me again?" Surprised by his politeness I don't answer right away. I nod and manage to get the words out. "Yes, I would like that."

"Are you available after school tomorrow? I could pick you up."

The thought of seeing him so soon after today makes me giddy inside. Captured by his gaze, I feel paralyzed and unable to look away. He steps closer. Our foreheads touch, and I'm staring at his lips. I want him to kiss me. He moistens his lips, and our lips touch. He opens his mouth, and so do I. He tastes as good as he smells, and I think I might faint. His hands slide down to my low back, but then he stops, and our lips part. He catches his breath and steps back.

My heart tries to recover. "Is something wrong?"

His hand touches his mouth. "I should head back."

He's acting strange about our kiss. Should I be embarrassed? "You've never kissed someone before?"

"Oh, yes, but I probably should have asked first."

"It's okay. I wanted you to kiss me, Victor."

He reaches Amanda's reigns and says, "See you tomorrow, after school."

He mounts Amanda and gallops away.

In Two Moons

Victor leads Amanda into her stall and unsaddles her. He brushes her back to remove the saddle marks. His thoughts about Anah bounce around in his mind. I shouldn't have kissed her so soon. I told myself to go slow but didn't. I don't want to seem typical. He looks straight into Amanda's eyes. Victor's mind is blown away from what he discovered from marking Anah. Is it possible?

The barn door opens, and Victor's father walks in. *"Is what possible?"* He transfers his thoughts to Victor and telepathically speaks to him.

"That I actually found a girl that I can relate to," says Victor while scraping mud out of Amanda's hoof.

"The ship will arrive in two moons, and you are to leave for your training." His father takes the saddle and places it with the others. *"It's too late to get involved, you know."*

"I think she's the one, Meirlies."

His father chuckles. *"I've heard that before, Minniedah. You've had plenty of time to find a mate, but now you must return to your training."*

Victor threw the pick into the bucket that holds grooming tools and brushes. "I'm going to see her again," he says out loud.

"Please, there's no reason to behave primally."

Victor resumes grooming. *"I just think this girl is special."*

"I can't stop you from seeing this primonKi, but when the time comes you will leave with the others." His father turns and leaves the barn.

Victor kept from his father what he possibly learned from Anah's kiss. He isn't sure yet what it means. Only that he has to be careful with this knowledge if it is actually true. It would only be a matter of time before his father realizes that he's keeping something from him. He's good at secrets, better than most Monahdah, but his father might pay attention.

Victor enters his room. It's carved out of the sandstone walls into an elaborate cave. Curved halls lead to rooms with beautiful hand carved pillars, windows and walls. Stairs lead to a secret passage that follows to the main house. The main house is shared by his father and other Monahdah that temporarily reside there. Victor's main contribution is cooking for the group. He doesn't mind this duty because he loves to cook. Eating is more of a pleasurable, social activity than a necessity.

The others will arrive soon. Monahdah will come here from southern New Mexico, Arizona, Utah and Colorado for the big event when we make the exchange. Many will leave Earth and migrate back to NeuMonah, and others will arrive. This place will be busy. He was looking forward to his departure and resuming his training. Now he anxiously waits for his next encounter with Anah.

He rests his head back on his reading chair and looks at his shelf full of literature he's collected while he's been on Earth. His eyes move to the *Mon* stone at the end of the shelf. The same stone that's in Anah's ring. He reaches for it and caresses the smooth, glass like surface. It glows brighter to his touch. Staring into the orange and red orb, he decides he will show Anah tomorrow. The first step of unveiling who he really is, and possibly who she really is. It's risky, and he would be going against the norm, but getting to know the truth about Anah will be worth it.

The Usual Table

I look up at the clock for the fiftieth time today. I see Victor in two hours. The minutes feel like hours. School is already so boring, and now that I actually have something to look forward to it's excruciating.

The bell rings for lunch, and I go to the usual table. Sophia is already there. She seems nervous when I arrive.

"Hey, Soph."

"Hey," she says, without looking at me.

"Why so glum?"

"Anah, I need to tell you something, and I'm afraid to tell you because you're my best friend, and I don't want you..."

"Just tell me. You're being silly." Suddenly I remember the way she hugged Tim after the concert Friday night and know what she's going to say. "Wait! Let me guess... you and Tim, right?"

"You're not mad?"

"Of course not. I saw the way you guys got along."

She hugs me. "You seem really into Victor, so I was hoping..."

"Speaking of which, he's picking me up today after school." I have a huge smile on my face.

"Oh my God!"

I open my milk carton. "I half expect to wake up from a dream."

"What are you guys gonna do?"

"I don't know. Yesterday he took me horseback riding, together on one horse— bareback."

"Get out!" she says too loudly. Tim sets his tray down on the table. "But I just got here."

"Hey, Tim," says Sophia clearing a space for him at the table. "We weren't talking to you."

Tim puts his arm around Sophia then asks, "What's all the excitement about?"

Sophia gives him a peck on the cheek. "Just girl talk."

I take my last bite of my macaroni and dare to look at the clock again.

Victor

The final bell rings, at last, and I bounce out of my chair. I play it cool because I don't want to look like some silly schoolgirl, even though I'm jumping around inside. I grab my coat from my locker, and maneuver my way through the crowded hallway to the exit doors.

There's a line full of buses in the bus lane. The sound of an engine comes from the other side of the bus and a shiny, black car pulls up to the curb. It's Victor, making a grand entrance, driving an old car that's making heads turn. I don't know anything about cars, but it's awesome. He opens the passenger door for me. "My queen," he says with a sparkle in his eyes. I sense everyone staring at us or the car. I climb in and recognize a mixture of scents: the car's black leather interior, Victor's sweet cinnamon scent, and roses. Roses? Victor reaches behind to the back seat and gives me not one, not two, but three dozen red, white and yellow roses. "I didn't know what color you like."

"Wow, Victor! I don't know what to say. I don't have a color preference. You could've picked one." I smell the roses. "Thank you!"

"You're welcome."

We cruise past the Plaza and busy tourists visiting the Indian vendors in front of the Palace of the Governors. It's a beautiful Santa Fe day, and the snow from the day before has vanished. The windows are down blowing my hair all around. Someone standing on the plaza whistles, impressed with car. "Cool car," says the man at the stop light. "Thanks," Victor says.

I put on my shades and ask, "What kind of car is it?"

"It's a 442 Oldsmobile from 1970." He turns down Old Pecos Trail and gets on the interstate. "Did you talk to your Mom about your father yet?"

"Not yet." I have to roll the window up manually with a handle. "Where are we going?"

"I thought you might want to see where I live."

"Sure." I decide that now's a good time to ask Victor some simple questions since I don't know much about him. "So, where do you go to school, Victor?"

"I don't."

"Oh, homeschooled?"

"Something like that," he says with a serious edge.

"Are you from around here?"

"I've only lived here for a year or so."

We're driving now on a long dirt road that winds up to the Glorieta mesa. "Wow, you really do live remotely."

We finally arrive at a gate. He rolls the window down to push in a code at a box, and the gate opens. "I feel like we're entering Area 51," I joke. Victor doesn't laugh though. "You know... secret government... conspiracies... captured aliens..."

"Yeah, I know what you mean."

We drive past a field where a couple of horses graze, and I recognize Amanda swishing away flies with her tail. He parks the car in a garage next to another antique car. "Your family likes old cars."

"My father... he has a thing for your 60's, 70's era."

"What do you mean, *my era?* I'm just seventeen, Victor."

"Oh, I didn't mean it that way. I'm Sorry." Victor's tension makes me uncomfortable. I'm wondering if this was a mistake.

"Is something wrong?"

He takes the keys out of the ignition and turns to me. He moves a strand of hair out of my face. "Come here," he says, and my heart skips a beat. I slide over next to him. He puts his arm around me and stares directly into my eyes. "I'm glad you're here, Anah. I've been looking forward to it all day," he says in a soothing tone that puts me back at ease.

Through a garden path we hold hands. I feel like I just stepped into a fairy tale. Chickens are pecking and scratching under an apple tree ripe with fruit. We laugh at his goat reaching up as far as his neck can stretch for an apple, even though there are several within his reach. There's an herb and flower garden where bees are busy at work gathering pollen. In the field are two small geometric wooden towers.

"What are those?" I gesture to the structures.

"Bee hives. We have three queen bees. The colonies provide a lot of honey for us. I'll let you try some later."

We come to a peculiar building. From the outside it looks like something Bilbo Baggins would live in. The walls are curved and look sculpted by hand. Interesting patterns of stones create a swirl design on the outside wall.

"Is this some kind of earth house?"

"Yes, I made it myself. I carved it out of the sandstone."

"This is like a work of art!" We walk through the passage ways of carved tunnels and pillars. "I mean, this is crazy!" His bed is also carved right out of the sandstone wall. There are circular windows and doors that allow light and shadows to display the carved designs and figures he has made on the walls. The floor is hard and smooth. His bed is in a cove with a circular mattress with lots of pillows along the wall. The only furniture is a cozy armchair that sits next to a big circular fixed window.

"Are your parents hippies?"

He laughs. "Not really. We just like things the natural way."

"Where are they?"

"My father is out for the afternoon. My mother doesn't live here. She lived in North Africa and died in a civil war. I never got to meet her."

"I'm sorry."

"It's okay."

"But I know what it's like to grow up without a parent. There's always a part of you that feels missing or cheated."

His thoughts seem to trail off. He looks directly at me, as if he has something serious to say or ask, something that's been on his mind since he picked me up at school. "Do you like school?"

I shrug my shoulders. "It's okay."

"You don't seem sure."

"Well, I didn't want to sound like a complainer." I glance over his book collection. "It pretty much sucks."

"Are you going to college?"

"That's the plan. Hopefully it will be more challenging."

"It may not be for you." He sits on the edge of his arm chair.

"You don't get bored with homeschooling?"

He has a puzzled look on his face. "Homeschooling?"

"You said you were homeschooled."

"It's boring sometimes and a little lonely."

"I think the only reason I get up and go to school is to be around people; although sometimes that can get tedious." I pick up a book by Rudolf Steiner titled, 'How to Know Higher Worlds.'

"I noticed at the concert that you're different from your friends."

I hold up his book as evidence. "And you're not?" I page through the book. "How do I seem different?"

"Well, do you think you're like everyone else?"

"When I make an effort to be like everyone else."

"You ignore who you are to be like them?"

This is turning into a strange conversation. "I guess I do."

"What capabilities do you have?"

I look at him sidelong. "Capabilities?"

"Others might think them to be supernatural gifts."

"I don't have any of those gifts," I lie like I was trained to do. I've learned to hide anything unexplained. If science has no explanation then it is unnatural, and you are a freak to society. Knowing when someone is not telling the truth or hearing voices, for instance, could land you in a mental hospital or on brain-numbing drugs. When I was twelve, my mother came home with a man. He was a real pervert, and I could hear him thinking about what he wanted to do with her sexually. While we ate, I tricked him into feeling sick with my thoughts. He became violently ill and had to leave. My mother constantly warned me as a child that people would take me away, and I would never see her again if I used these "tricks." Out of fear, I've blocked every "unnatural" capability that I developed, so I don't want to tell him how I heard his thoughts and freak him out. But why is he asking about this?

"Hmm," he sighs and walks to his bookshelf. "I want to show you something." He's about to retrieve something but something distracts him, and he peers out the big round window.

"What is it?" I ask.

"My father... he's calling me."

"Should we go see what he wants?"

"It's not necessary." He looks at me with those light aqua marine eyes. I sense a sudden shift in mood. "Let's talk more later."

"You were going to show me something."

"That can wait."

I'm relieved his mood has lightened up. He sits down on his cozy armchair with a sigh. "You'll have to go soon, and..."

"And, what?" I don't need telepathy to know what he's thinking. His eyes beckon me to come closer. I sit on his lap, and he caresses my face.

"You don't have to pretend around me, Anah." He tucks a loose strand of hair behind my ear. "I want you to be yourself."

There's something hypnotic about being in his presence. He puts his hand firmly behind my neck and draws me close to him. We kiss. It's a deeper, hungrier kiss than before, and I can feel his heart pounding against my chest. As if I'm under a state of hypnosis, I lose track of everything, and we melt into each other's arms. My movements are less voluntary, and it feels good to lose control.

A tall and very large man who looks a lot like Victor steps into the room. He stands there a moment, and then finally says, "You have company." I stand up quickly, looking clumsy. "You must be Anah."

Cool as a cucumber, Victor introduces me. "Anah, this is my father."

"I'm sorry. I didn't mean to sneak up on you like that." He gives Victor a hard look. "I came to tell you that a meeting begins after dinner." Astoundingly, he continues his conversation telepathically, and I listen. *"Monahdah from Roswell will arrive soon. Your promptness is expected."*

Victor answers respectfully, *"Thank you, Meirlies, for your news."*

"Victor was getting ready to take me home." I grab my coat from the bed. I'm confused and embarrassed for hearing them telepathically communicate.

"It was nice to meet you, Anah," he says as he disappears back into the maze of tunnels. I feel relief when he leaves. His physical presence is overwhelming, and I'm not sure if he likes my being here.

Victor gets up, wraps his arms around me, and playfully tackles me to the bed. "Now, where were we?" He kisses my neck.

"Victor, I think he wants me to go." I nudge him away.

"Don't let him frighten you. He's all bark and no bite, as they say." He kisses my neck again.

I ignore his playful attempts because I'm too distracted by the fact that I allowed myself to hear their thoughts. More importantly, I heard Victor and his father have a telepathic conversation! Perhaps I'm not as unique as I thought. I decide to use caution and not disclose this.

"What kind of meeting do you have to go to?"

"A family meeting, I guess you could call it." He kisses me on the lips.

Shadows shift across the room on the floor and walls of the white sandstone. I look out the round window. "I should head back. It's getting dark." I break away from his spell.

"I'll take you to your house."

"You can just take me to The Roadrunner." I put on my coat. "I really want to talk to my mom, anyway."

"About your father?"

I look at my phone to check the time. "Oh, damn. She already left. I guess you'll have to drive me all the way back."

"I don't mind. That just means we get to spend more time together." He puts his arm around me.

I have a lot of thoughts swimming around in my mind, like the strange conversation we had before our make out session. Now I feel paranoid that he can read my mind.

Victor takes my hand and says, "I hope we can spend more time together before..."

"Before what?"

"Well, before you go to college."

He was thinking something else, but I'm afraid to probe into his mind without him probing back.

We pull into my driveway. "Do you want to come in?"

"I'll greet your mother," he says, and I laugh.

"What do you find humorous?"

"You talk like you're reading a book."

"I forget that people here speak differently than they write."

"Where do they not do that?" He ignores my question and opens the passenger door for me. He's also more gentlemanly than other guys I know.

"Hi, Mom," I say walking through the door.

"I just left you a voice mail," she says. Her face lights up when she sees Victor. "Hi, Victor. Are you hungry? I have some pasta in the oven."

I sense she's being nice but wants to avoid any conversation with me about my father. Victor knows this. I'm much more intuitive at home since it's my safe environment. However, since I met Victor, I'm unusually sensitive as if a weight is slowly lifting off my chest. That doesn't explain the telepathic conversation between him and his father though.

"I would like that very much, but I have to meet my father."

"Okay. Maybe next time then."

Victor kisses me goodbye and whispers in my ear, "See you soon."

Double Date

"So how was your day with mystery man?" asks Sophia.

I'm quiet at the lunch table since I'm consumed by my thoughts of my strange visit with Victor yesterday. "It was good." I didn't sound convincing enough.

Sophia raises a brow. "Out with it. What's wrong?"

"Nothing." I take a bite of my pizza. I can't tell her, of course, that I heard a telepathic conversation between my boyfriend and his father.

Tim sets his lunch tray on the table and plops down without saying anything. I make an attempt to redirect the conversation. "What are you two up to this weekend?"

"We should all get together," says Sophia, nudging Tim.

"You mean, like, double date?" Tim sounds unenthusiastic.

"Sure, why not?" Sophia scowls.

"I'll ask Victor, and see if he's into it."

"Yes, I would like to join you," says Victor's voice. I quickly pivot around in my chair. Holy crap. I must be crazy. I mean really frickin' crazy.

Sophia and Tim stare at me quizically. "Anah, what's with you?"

"Nothing...I thought I heard.... never mind."

Sophia continues with a plan. "We could meet at the lake. It's supposed to be really warm. A good excuse to wear my new bikini."

"Okay...that sounds fun."

"Cool. Saturday at noon, if that's cool." Sophia says. "Oh, I can't wait!" She hugs Tim with excitement.

I stand up from the lunch table and swing my backpack on. "I'll see you later."

"Okay, see you later," says Soph. "See ya," Tim says with his mouth full of his sandwich.

I head straight for the bathroom and stand before the mirror. I stare at my reflection. I think back to my strange conversation with Victor when he asked me if I had any supernatural abilities. Can you hear me? I close my eyes, and suddenly I can hear the thoughts of someone in the bathroom stall, and the thoughts of people walking by the bathroom. The thoughts of teachers in the teachers' lounge on the other side of the wall. Overwhelmingly, I hear the thoughts of everyone in the school! I cover my ears, and I'm found in the corner of the bathroom, crouched down on the floor.

"Are you okay? Do you want me to get someone?" asks the girl who was in the bathroom stall.

"No. No, thank you. I'm just…I'm fine." I say as I stand up and pat cold water on my face.

"Are you sure?"

"Yes, I'm fine now. I'm sorry if I scared you."

Satisfied, she turns and leaves the bathroom.

Jump

The bathroom incident yesterday at school is embarrassing. Thank God, there was only one witness. Today is a new day with myself and my friends, including Victor. Reflecting back on it, it feels like I wasn't me. I'll move on like it didn't happen, knowing that I'm stronger than before, and it's only human to sometimes feel overcome with stress. That's why I turned off this ability before, and when I let it trickle back in it burst in like a flood. I'm grateful Sophia wasn't there to see my temporary loss of sanity. If I had knowledge of why I am the way I am then I could perhaps not react so strongly next time. If there is a next time. Hopefully there's not.

I hear the unmistakable sound of Victor's Oldsmobile pull into the driveway. I called him earlier, and he's excited about the day trip to the lake.

I notice a basket in the back seat as I get in. "What's that for?"

"I packed some food and drinks," he says as I stare at him with admiration and give him a kiss. "That's very thoughtful, and it's really cool of you to agree to this. You know, hanging out with me and my friends."

Like a blue emerald in the middle of the desert, we see the lake. We pull into the makeshift dirt parking lot and park next to Sophia's car. Victor grabs the basket and a blanket from the backseat.

Sophia is sporting a bikini and lies on a blanket spread out on the red rock. Tim lies on his side next to her.

"How's the water?" I ask to announce our arrival.

"Hey! You made it!" Sophia says in her high-pitched voice. She gets up and hugs me.

"Guys, this is Victor. Victor, this is Sophia and Tim." Victor shakes hands with Tim. Tim averts his eyes. Victor stands much taller than him, and I sense a moment of intimidation. Tim isn't a huge guy to begin with, and I realize in that moment that he's self conscious about his height. Tim lights up a cigarette.

Victor and I spread out the blanket on the warm red boulder.

"Did you go in the lake yet?" Victor asks.

"Crazy?" Sophia takes a drag from the cigarette. "It's way too cold." She lies back on the blanket and exhales the smoke.

"There's a place where you can jump off," says Victor.

"Yeah, it's a fifty foot jump. Everyone does it at least once before they graduate," says Tim flicking his cigarette.

"Have you ever jumped?" Sophia asks Tim.

"No, but maybe I will today."

"Maybe we all should," says Victor.

"No way," Sophia says putting up her hand in protest. "I don't know what's in that water. Besides, I don't have anything to prove to you dimwits." Tim passes the cigarette back to her, and she takes another drag.

"I'm in," says Tim exhaling. "Anah?"

"I don't think so. I didn't bring a suit."

Victor points. "That trail over there leads to the cliff."

I'm not sure what it is about boys and showing each other up.

"Let's go then." Tim holds the cigarette between his lips, takes off his jeans and stands there in his underwear. "Who says you need a suit?"

Victor removes his jeans. "Right behind you." Then he pulls off his shirt revealing a big tattoo on his back, a geometric design of interlocking triangles.

Sophia puts on her sneakers. "Wait, I'm coming."

We climb to the top of the trail and arrive at the jump off place. Tim stares down. He's having second thoughts. "Fifty feet doesn't sound as high as it looks." Tim folds his arms in front of his chest and takes a step back.

Victor pats him on the shoulder. "Don't worry. You'll land in approximately 1.7 seconds. That's nothing."

"How do you know?"

Sophia rolls her eyes. "Tim, he's doing the math."

"Based on your planet's... I mean, the Earth's gravitational pull, the rate of speed for a free falling object is about 32 feet per second." He steps up to the edge. "Just follow my lead."

"Let's jump together." I surprise myself by my outburst and elevated adrenaline. I remove my dress, which isn't a big deal since I'm wearing a matching black bra and underwear.

"Anah, don't leave me up here," Sophia whines.

I grab Victor's hand as if to seize the moment before I change my mind.

"On the count of three." Victor counts, "One... two," he clasps my hand tightly, "three!" We fly through the air, and before I have the chance to scream we're submerged in water. Our hands unclasp as we swim back up to the surface. I swim up for air and yell out with excitement.

"Are you okay?" Sophia hollers.

I look at Sophia and Tim. "That was incredible, Sophia. You gotta do it!"

"Where's Victor?" Tim yells.

I spin around but don't see him anywhere. "He didn't come up? He should have come up!" I dive underwater and open my eyes, but I can't see anything. I resurface for air and dive back down again. This time I go deeper but still don't see anything other than rocks and dirt. A small fish darts away before I swim back to the surface. I yell up to them on the cliff, "Do you see him?" They both stand there dumbfounded. "Victor!" I scream out across the empty lake. Victor splashes me with water. "Here I am."

"Victor, what the hell! Where were you?"

"Swimming. Isn't that what you're supposed to do when you're in water?" he splashes me again. "Come on down," he yells up the cliff. "The water's perfect!"

"Come on! The water's not too cold." I splash Victor in the face to get him back. We start chanting, "Jump, jump, jump."

Sophia and Tim stand at the edge of the cliff holding their hands together in the air as we continue chanting. Victor and I swim off to the side, and we hear a scream and a plunge into the water. They come up, and all of us are screaming, laughing, and hollering like monkeys.

"Sophia, you did it. You really did it!"

"I know! I really did! But you lied. This water's freakin' cold! Is my mascara running?"

"Yes, all over. It's a good look for you. Like one of those sad models." I bust up laughing. We swim to the edge of the lake and run back wet and cold to our blankets.

After we dry off, and our adrenaline settles, we eat and share our snacks; Victor's homemade bread with a delicious tomato and basil spread, made from the tomatoes in his garden, and Sophia's strawberries. It's turning into an awesome day, and I'm feeling happy with my friends, one of the best feelings in the world.

Tim turns to Victor. "Where are you from? I've never seen you around."

"I've lived here for about a year."

"Where did you move from?"

Victor looks relaxed and normal, but he's experiencing some discomfort because he has to lie. Why, I don't know.

"Wisconsin. My father farmed there. He's also an antique dealer specializing in old cars."

"Oh, that explains the cool car you have."

"Was that your first jump?" Sophia says as she curls up close to Tim under a blanket.

"I come here often, actually. I'm not used to the dryness." A bead of water drips from Victor's nose.

"Where were you... that whole time you disappeared?" Tim asks.

Victor takes a strawberry. "Underwater."

Sophia's eyes open wide. "How could've you been under water for that long?"

"That wasn't long," he says as he bites into a juicy strawberry. "It's something I practice."

Tim rubs Sophia's back to warm her and says, "So how long can you hold your breath for?"

Victor sucks the juice from his thumb. "If I tell you, you won't believe me."

"Victor, I'm going to go back up the trail to get my dress." I wrap a blanket tightly around me. Victor takes my hand as we head back up the trail. I want to ask Victor what he's hiding, but I don't feel comfortable yet to be confrontational. I haven't come clean about my ability to read minds yet, and I don't want him to know that I heard him and his father having a telepathic conversation.

I stare at the tattoo on his back instead. "What's that symbol? The tattoo on your back?"

"It's a yantra. It symbolizes unity in the universe."

He picks up my dress and sits down on a boulder. I like the way he looks against the red rocks with his skin glowing gold in the setting sun.

"Excuse me, sir. My dress please."

"Come and get it," he teases. I raise my eyebrow at him and walk over. He's sitting, so we're at eye level. His eyes light up with a hunger that sets my heart on fire. Goosebumps cover my body with the sensation of his touch. His skin and hands are warm, almost hot, as they squeeze me closer to him. He does that thing with his lips before he gets ready to kiss me, and my heart shoots out electric waves of desire. He kisses me tenderly yet passionately. His hands explore my back and now the back of my thighs. His legs are on either side of me, and he presses them against me. Making out with Victor is like a drug. It has strange power over me. I'm not sure I like the feeling of losing control. It's not a feeling I'm acquainted with. I understand how the brain works and the releasing of chemicals. Dopamine, for example, is a powerful chemical in the brain that can make you feel infatuated, but I feel there's a stronger force at work here.

I hear voices coming up the trail, and a small group of boys from my high school are standing at the edge of the cliff.

"Get a room!" One of them yells at us.

"Yeah--jump or get out!" they tease.

I slip my dress over my head and yell, "Same goes for you! Jump or get out!" One of them jumps backwards into a beautiful back dive. The other two jump in yelling profanities on the way down before they make a loud plunge into the water.

Then I get the courage. "Victor? Did you lie to Tim?"

"About what?"

"Maybe it's none of my business, but when he asked you where you were from I had the feeling you were lying when you said Wisconsin."

"Why do you think I lied?"

"It was just a feeling. You know. A very normal feeling that you were hiding something."

"Didn't you tell me that you didn't have any special abilities?"

"I just want us to be honest with each other. That's all."

He stands and seems taller than usual. "So do I."

Darn, I'm terrible at confrontations. He's hiding something from me though, and I don't want to make a big deal of it. "I'm sorry. It was silly of me to think you were lying about where you were from." I want to take it back and replace the awkward silence with making out. Plus, he's right. I haven't been honest myself.

"One more jump?" he asks, taking off his jeans.

"I'll pass."

Victor runs to the edge and with a swift leap into the air, he bends his body with perfection, clasping his feet, and does one flip before unfolding into a perfect dive.

Gem Store

It's 1:00 a.m. I open my bedside table drawer and take out the box I keep the ring in. I stare at it glowing in the darkness. I like to watch it swirl orange and red when I touch it. The repeated image of the man holding me as a child flashes in my mind again. Perhaps I really do have a stored memory of my father.

I'm really curious about this stone. I think it's a clue about my father. Tomorrow I'll take it to the gem store and ask someone about its origin and where it could be from. Maybe that will provide me with some answers.

In the morning, I drop Mom off at work and follow the directions on my phone to the Natural Stone store. I'm led down Baca Street to a small warehouse. I walk into a room full of rocks and gems that are somewhat organized in boxes of many rows and on several tables.

"Hello," says a man peaking over his black plastic framed glasses. "Are you joining our class today?"

"I'm just looking for someone who can identify a stone that I have." I reach into my bag and retrieve the box.

"You've come to the right place." He removes a box from a table and places it on the floor. "Let's see what you've got." He holds the ring between his index finger and thumb, turning it one way then another. I notice that the colors don't swirl or glow the way they normally do when I'm holding it. He looks back at me curiously, and I dial into his thoughts. I use caution this time, so I don't repeat what happened to me in the bathroom at school. He's surprised that he doesn't have any idea what kind of stone it is and doesn't want to embarrass himself, so he decides to lie.

He puts a magnifying glass over his eye as if to get a closer look. He glances at me with a reassuring smile. *"This is some crazy shit. What the hell is this?"*

"You don't know what it is?" I stare back.

He takes off the glasses and studies the stone with his naked eye. "Where did you get this?"

"My-I mean... I found it."

"I'm pretty sure its citron." He walks over to a locked box and takes out another small box. "Look at this." He hands me a pretty, orange stone. "They come in different shades of orange and yellow."

"Yeah, but when I hold yours, it doesn't change color and brighten. The one in my ring does." I demonstrate holding them together.

He gives me a funny look. "I've never seen that before."

Two people walk in through the door. "Our class is going to start if you would like to join us."

"Thanks, but I've got to go." I head for the door. "Thanks for your time."

"Hey umm... if you want, you could go to The Trading Post. Maybe someone there will know."

"Where's that?"

"In the village of Cerrillos."

Los Cerrillos

I'm a forty minute drive from the village but decide it's worth the extra gas. The last time I was in Cerrillos was in seventh grade. We went there on a school field trip to learn about the history of New Mexico. The teacher was so passionate about the town's history that he transported me, for a moment, back in time. I remember a man stumbling out of the saloon waving his pistol around at another man and a woman dressed in period clothing. I was frightened and warned the teacher because I thought it was really happening, that everyone could surely see this goaded, drunken man ranting in anger ready to fire his pistol. He was convinced that the man was having an affair with his wife. The wife was screaming for him to put the gun down. The drunk man fired his weapon, and I crouched down in fear of getting shot. The class snickered at me, and the teacher ignored my plea to leave the area. When I looked back, the event was over, and no one was there. I realized I was witnessing an event long past. Several kids called me a freak, and freak became my nickname that seventh grade year. Sophia grabbed my arm and told me to forget it. That was the day we became friends.

The teacher continued to talk about how the town was the oldest mining town in the U.S. The Indians mined turquoise here over a thousand years ago. Some of the crown jewels of Spain are adorned with the turquoise from these mines dug up by Spanish miners. Early Europeans set up camp in these hills in the 1500's when silver and lead and other precious metals were discovered underneath them. It wasn't until 1879 when Colorado miners swarmed the hills. With a new train station, church and school, a bustling town was born nearly overnight.

Now the dogs don't even want to get out of the dirt-covered streets as I drive through, and I have to stop. I wait, but he doesn't move. I need to actually get out of the car to ask the napping dog to get out of the way. He lazily looks at me and reluctantly gets up. He walks about three feet and plops down again. I manage to drive around him. Driving through the sleepy western town, I imagine what it was like during its heyday with shops selling the miners dreams of gold and silver with their pickets and shovels, and spending their earnings in the evenings in the saloons and brothels lining the dirt covered streets.

I park at the end of the dirt road that overlooks a large basin. I'm the only one here and don't see anyone around. The sign on the door says open. The bells hanging on the door announce my arrival as I walk into the old hacienda, but there's no one inside to greet me. Boxes of rocks, gem stones, and locally made jewelry cover the tables. Large chunks of turquoise adorn the stone fireplace in the corner of the room.

"Let me know if you would like to go into the museum," says a low, quiet voice. An old Native American man appears out of no where and stands right behind me. He's tall, like a statue, with long silver braids, and wearing turquoise necklaces, rings and bracelets. "Sorry, I didn't mean to startle you."

"Oh... that's okay. I actually came here to see if someone could help me identify this stone I brought."

"Sure," says a woman behind the counter. She's an old Anglo woman with long, shiny silver hair parted down the middle. She puts on her spectacles and examines the glowing gem. Her almond eyes look to the man who's now standing next to her. They exchange a few words in another language, some Native American tongue. She turns to look back at me. "Who made this?"

"I don't know. I found it."

"Where did you find it?"

I didn't want to say that my father gave it to me, and I didn't have a story prepared.

"It's okay, sweetie. You don't have to tell me anything you don't want to," she says with a soft raspy voice.

"Have you seen it before?"

They again have a side conversation in the other language. Through telepathy, I understand that they're talking about the ring and whether it's the same as something else. "I never have," she says emphasizing I. "Perhaps some scientist made it. You never know what they're making at the labs in Los Alamos. You should ask someone there."

That might be an idea. Maybe my Dad is a scientist living in Los Alamos. "Thanks for the advice." I put the ring back into my bag.

I pick up a turquoise bead out of a basket. "How much is this?"

She looks at the basket of beads. "That one is a dollar-fifty."

"And the leather cord?"

"Two dollars a foot."

I buy the turquoise and black leather cord and give her the exact amount.

"Good luck with your ring," she says as I walk out the door.

"Thanks."

I'm about to close the door to my car when I hear the low voice again. "Don't go to Los Alamos."

How does he sneak up on me like that? "What's that?"

"You won't find what you're looking for in Los Alamos," he says standing right next to my car door.

I wait for more information from him, but he just walks away. "Excuse me! Sir?" I get out of the car. He turns to face me, and we stare at each other, eye to eye. I didn't try to read his thoughts. I didn't want to pry, but it came as easily as my next breath. He thought if I went to Los Alamos my life would be in danger. He has seen the stone in my ring before. What I saw next was murky so I ask, "Can you tell me? Where you saw this stone before?"

He pointed. I look out over the mass of space in the basin to where he might be pointing. "Out there? In the desert?"

"There was a crash." He looks up at the sky recalling the image. "It looked like a car or a truck on fire falling from the sky. It was dark but the moon was bright. I walked in that direction," he pointed with his eyes, "and found it."

I know what he's going to say, but I ask anyway. "Found what?"

"A star ship. Most would call it a UFO. It crashed, and there was debris everywhere."

"What happened to it?"

"Well, when I went back to the crash site with my brother it was gone."

"And you saw this stone there?"

"It was inside the ship, a large tablet. It was the same, I'm sure."

"No bodies?"

"There was a star man. He was in bad shape. I went to get my brother for help. But when we got there everything was gone. We searched and searched. It was all gone."

"Maybe it was Los Alamos testing a new plane... some new technology."

"I wouldn't go there to find out."

"You didn't tell anyone?"

"I was eight years old. Most people thought I was making it up. That is, until the report came out about the crash in Roswell. There were other crashes too. Most people have only heard about the Roswell one."

A gust of wind whips up a cloud of dirt from the street. I close my eyes and shield my face from the impact of blowing dust. "Thanks for sharing your story." When I open my eyes, he's gone.

Manipulation

The Roadrunner is warm from the kitchen. I see Victor in the parking lot through the steamy windows, and we make eye contact. I draw a smily face on the glass. My heart beats with anticipation. As soon as he enters the restaurant the ladies that work here coo over him like a bunch of doves. A young waitress we nicknamed Bean, because she's so tall and thin, quickly puts on a fresh layer of lip balm. He sits next to me and greets me with an intoxicatingly sweet kiss. He leans back a few inches and looks at my lips. "I thought about that all day." He puts his arm around me. "But is something wrong?"

"Why do you ask?"

"You just seem bothered."

"I guess I had a weird day."

Mom sets down two glasses of water. "Are you two going to order?"

"Yeah, sure." I order my favorite, mac and cheese. Victor orders a salad then guzzles the water until it's gone. "What kind of weird day?"

"First, I was at the gem store, and the gem specialist said the stone in my ring was citron."

"You wanted it to be a ruby?"

"He wasn't telling the truth. The truth is he has no idea."

"Maybe he really thought it was citron."

"He was lying through his teeth."

"How do you know?" He stares directly into my eyes.

"Because…" I was about to blurt out that I could read his mind. "I just could tell, Victor." I take a sip of my water. "Then I went to Cerrillos, and this Native American man—"

"Here you are, Victor. One house salad." Mom lays down our plates. "And for you, macaroni and cheese."

"Thanks Mom."

Victor picks up his fork. "He recognized your ring… this man?"

"Well, yes." I stare at the heat rising from my macaroni. "Don't you find that strange?"

"That he recognized the stone?"

"No, that you know what I'm going to say, sometimes before I do?"

"Lucky guess… but please, continue your story about your weird day."

I take a deep breath. "He said that he saw a space ship crash out in the desert. It would have been in 1947. He saw the same kind of stone inside this space ship! He went back to the crash site with his brother and everything was gone, including the 'star man' that was injured, maybe dead."

"And you think that's weird?"

"You don't?"

"Sounds like Roswell. In fact, that happened the same year."

"Yeah! All the weirder." I take a bite of my macaroni.

"It should be an interesting conversation with your Mom about this connection between your father, the ring and this spaceship. Don't you think?"

"Yeah, but it gets weirder. I want to go to Los Alamos to see if maybe my father has some connection there. You know, maybe he's a scientist and this mysterious stone is his handiwork. But the man warned me not to go there."

With a serious look of concern, Victor says, "Don't go there. His advice is wise."

"How do you mean?"

"Just talk to your mother first and see what she has to say. She'll tell you what you need to know, if you just ask. If you want, I could help you have the conversation with her about it."

"That's sweet of you to offer, but you don't have to get involved in my personal matters."

"I feel that your matters are my matters," he says looking at me with those aquamarine eyes.

"That's okay. I know what I have to do."

"You mean to get her to open up?"

"It's something I haven't done since I was ten years old, and I vowed I would never do it again."

"Manipulation?"

"I prefer the word persuasion."

"How would you do it?"

Mom comes over to the table and takes her apron off. "I'm ready to go whenever you are."

Victor kisses me goodbye. "I'll see you soon."

"Bye, Victor," says Mom. "Are you going to finish that?" She gestures at my plate. "You can have it." I slide it over to her. "Why don't you sit down, Mom, and give your feet a rest?"

"Okay," she sighs. "Victor didn't have to go on my account."

I get right to the point. "Mom, tell me about my dad."

She stops chewing for a moment. "What do you want to know? I've already told you everything."

"No, you haven't." I use my 'tricks' and tell her to tell me everything she knows and to reconnect to memories that are blocked.

"I don't remember much." She takes a bite of my food. "In fact, if you weren't born, then I might not remember anything. I do remember some of it but not much."

I narrow my eyes at her. "What do you mean, if I wasn't born? If I wasn't born you wouldn't remember anything?"

She leans forward and whispers. "They have a way of making you forget."

I lean closer to her. "They?"

"When your father courted me, I was eighteen. It felt like I was on a drug, or like I was under a spell when I was with him. I know this sounds silly, but I can tell you. You're not a little girl anymore." She hesitates and looks around the room. I encourage her in my mind, and she continues. "He made me feel trust and removed stress and fear from my mind. It was like he—"

"He seduced you and took advantage of you it sounds like! Then he left you and me."

"Lower your voice. I know what it sounds like but—"

"That's sure what it sounds like to me."

"He was gentle and very kind, and he called me his queen. I loved him." She gazes out the window. "I still love him."

A sudden jolt surges through my body. Victor calls me that. Is this a strange coincidence?

"Where does he live? Is he a scientist in Los Alamos?"

"We shouldn't talk about it here." She looks around paranoid again. "They could be here," she whispers.

"Who are they?" I emphasize *they* again. "What the hell are you talking about?"

"I'll tell you more later," she says, clearing the plate of food into a to-go box. "Not here."

"Then where?"

"On the way home."

You Remember

The sunset stretches across the New Mexico sky behind the Jemez Mountains. The swirling colors of orange and red and hues of pink remind me of my ring lying in my purse. My life is on the cusp of something new, and that something will determine my future. Is my future in my hands? I don't believe in fate. I do believe in missed opportunities, so I want to recognize an opportunity when it presents itself. I'm ready to know the truth about my father. I'm ready to know the truth about who I am.

I remove the ring from my bag, and the stone creates a soft glow in my hand. "I've done some research on this little guy. I looked online. I went to a gem store in town. Went to Cerrillos. As far as I can tell, this stone doesn't exist. So what the hell is it?" I glance over at her to see her reaction. You will tell me what you know, I think to myself. I concentrate hard. She thinks she's forgotten, but I know I can get her to retrieve her memories if I convince her that she remembers. "Mom, you remember. Your memories are there. I'm not afraid, and neither should you be. I'm no longer a child, like you said. I think it's safe to talk now, Mom."

She takes the ring from my hand and admires it. "It's not safe. That's why I've never talked about it. He told me I had to be careful."

"Who?"

"Your father." She takes a deep breath.

I pull the car over onto the side of the road and wait. I cross my arms. I'm not going anywhere until she tells me what she knows.

"He's not from here. He got that ring…" Her voice trails off. "Honey," she taps her fingernail on the armrest of the door. I finally hear what she's about to say but has been unable to tell me for seventeen years. "He comes from another planet."

I let that sink in for a moment. I finally find the giant puzzle piece, and I'm unable to put it into the picture. "You think there are more walking around?"

"You wouldn't know it if they were because they look just like us, except they're far advanced. They can heal themselves. I think they can even make themselves look different if they need to. They're like perfect beings."

"Are you? Are you one of them?"

"No, no," she quietly chuckles, "I'm far from perfect, but…" She looks at me.

"But I am."

"Yes." She lets out a giant exhalation like a huge weight has been removed off of her chest and she can breathe again.

"Why did he want you to be so cautious about me?"

"I don't know. I think that's why I'm made to forget. I think it's important for you to behave as if you don't know anything, also."

"That should be easy. I can't imagine going around telling people that I'm not exactly human. So where is he then?"

"Not in Los Alamos."

I look up at the earliest signs of night and the brightest stars are shining. "You don't know where he is?"

"I wish I knew."

"What was he...or what were *they* doing here?"

"I think they come here to..."

"To what?"

"I'm not sure, but I think they come here to procreate."

"Oh my God! That's awesome!" I shake my head in disgust. "They just use us to procreate, and we don't have any say?"

"I'm not sure, Anah, but you can't tell anyone this."

My head feels light and faint. Thoughts swirl around in my head. "There must be others like me then... hybrids?"

"I never concerned myself with that. Keeping you safe and out of the hands of people who would pick your brain apart or your body...." She catches her breath. "Losing you was my worst nightmare and still is."

I look at her as if it's the first time and realize how much I love the strong, beautiful person she is. I move over and hug her. "I love you, Mommy."

"I love you, too."

I don't know if the love I feel right now is human or alien, but feeling it is comforting. I'm relieved I can still feel this way inside.

"One more thing." I caress the steering wheel. "Could he hear your thoughts?"

"Yes, he could. He always knew what I was going to say or do, even before I did." She clutches her purse tight. "I know you can, too."

"It drove me crazy to hear everyones thoughts' day and night, without a break. I learned how to turn it off. So don't feel embarrassed when you're reading your book."

Mom grips her purse. "You control it?"

"Not entirely, but yeah. That's why I would sit by the creek for very long periods of time. I needed a place to escape from all the noise in my head. " I take back the ring. "Since this has come into my life, I feel awake. Like I was seeing in black and white, but now I see in color and in HD. And sometimes I hear..." I stop myself from telling her about Victor and the strange phenomena of hearing him speak telepathically with his father.

"You hear what?"

"Nothing. I'm just adjusting to this. To all of this."

"I'm sorry for any trouble this has been for you. Don't take this the wrong way, but I don't regret being with your father."

"I know. It's okay. I wish I knew more about him."

The sunset is complete and darkness blankets the mountains and valleys. Twilight hangs over Santa Fe. Dimly lit windows shine in the valley below, and we go home.

The Dark Starry Night

I try to concentrate on my school project to keep my mind focused on other things besides the fact that I'm only half human and half, well, I don't know what the other half is. The project isn't due until the end of the school year, but why procrastinate when I can get this done tonight. We can choose any subject, so I'm doing it on bees.

I can't believe this is actually real. Does the government know aliens live here? I take the ring out of the box. This is a gift from my father, my alien father. That explains the stone at least. It's not from this planet, probably his. It doesn't explain what the hell they're doing here, though, or what they want. If they come here to breed, then I can't be the only one. There must be others. I make up my mind. I'll go to Los Alamos and do some digging. The warning to not go there has only stirred my curiosity even more.

And then there's Victor, the telepathic conversation he had with his father, the times I thought I heard him speak to me without speaking, and all the times he knew what I was thinking. What about the fact that he's been so interested in my ring?

On my desk sits a bowl of stuff, like paperclips, erasers, etc., and I fish out one of the tacks. I push the tack through the dermis of my index finger and stare at the blood oozing out of the puncture. It looks like blood. It's not green, anyway. What did I expect? I've seen my blood before when I crashed my mountain bike into a boulder. My knee bled profusely. By the time I washed the blood off in the creek, the cut was gone. I suck the red dot from my finger, and a knock at my window makes me jump out of my seat.

Victor stands outside the window. "Victor, you scared the shit out of me. Why didn't you just use the door?" I ask as he climbs into my room.

"I didn't want to disturb your mom." He gives me a hug. Tension and stress melt away as I smell his warm scented skin. I recall what Mom said about my dad— 'He made me feel trust and removed stress and fear from my mind,' and I step away.

He looks confused. "What is it?"

I cross my arms. "Nothing, why?"

He gives me a puzzled stare, and I can hear his thoughts. The signal gets stronger. He wants to tell me the truth about something. He sits down on the bed, and I notice he's wearing a brown wool satchel across his chest. "What's in the bag?"

"Something I've been wanting to show you." He removes the strap over his head. "Your mother told you about your father..."

"How do you know that?"

"I just know.... It's something I want to...."

This ignites my distrust even more. "Like you could tell that your horse wanted to graze at that spot in the woods?"

"Yes."

"And how you knew I wanted the pepper and not the salt before I asked?"

"Yes, and just how *you* knew that man was lying to you about what kind of stone is in your ring. Anah, aren't you tired? Tired of pretending that you don't know what's going on?"

I narrow my eyes at him. "Why do you call me your queen?"

"Anah, you're upset. Maybe I should come back another time."

Mom told me to act like I don't know anything about my dad. I'm nervous because I don't know whom I can trust. How do I know I can trust Victor?

"I don't think this is a good time," he says as he puts the strap of his satchel back over his head.

I nervously look at his bag. "What is it that you want to show me?"

He reaches inside his bag and pulls out a large sphere about the size of a fortune-teller's ball. My dim room glows orange and red. "That's the same stone as my ring, isn't it?"

"Yes."

"But why did you tell me you've never seen it before?"

"That's not exactly a lie," he says, "I've just never seen it here before. It's a Mon stone."

"Mon? So, where did you get it?"

"It's from the planet Mon... and so am I."

I'm pretty sure I heard him say what I think he said. "You're from another planet?"

"I wanted to tell you sooner, but..."

"What the hell do you want from me?"

"What do you mean?"

"You want to get me pregnant, don't you? Then you'll disappear leaving me stranded with a baby, like my father did." I'm freaking out and raising my voice.

"Anah, please."

"I want you to leave!"

He stares at me with those sultry eyes, and suddenly I feel like I'm on a runaway train watching it crash.

"You don't want to see me anymore?" There's a long awkward pause. I don't know who or what I'm mad at anymore.

"I want you to leave and never come back here." I want to take it back, but it's too late. The train has already crashed. I'm confused with mixed emotions of fear and anger, anger that suddenly seems unfairly directed at him. He turns and goes back out the way he came in, from the dark starry night. I burst into tears.

Sorting Out The Truth

Birds are singing loudly outside my window. I stayed awake the entire night. I take in a deep breath and smell Victor as if he's still in my room. Tingles spread over my skin.

My mind is blown away. Is this really happening? My father who left me is an alien, a being from another planet, and so is my boyfriend. I knew Victor was hiding something, but this? In my confusion and lack of trust I pushed him away. I don't know who or what to trust. How can I be frightened of someone I still long to be near? Not having answers about any of this was easier than sorting out the truth.

A tingling sensation in my chest sends a vibrational force into my ears. *"We need to talk."*

"Victor? You can hear me?"

"Yes, just like you can hear me."

I can't always have Victor listening in on me. I have to separate or block my thoughts. Like changing a radio transmission, I change the channel.

"Please, Anah, we need to talk."

Undetected

"Minniedah." Victor's father, AmanKi, has been addressing him. "Victor!" He uses his Earth name. Victor blinks, shifting his eyes back into focus and looks at his father.

"You're in charge of the food and planning the meals," repeats AmanKi.

"For how many this time?"

"Plan for one hundred."

"That's a lot of breeders."

"They're not coming to breed."

"There's been a breach," says Sahn, from Roswell, New Mexico. *"Simerin have a station."*

"They're stationed in this sector?" Victor communicates telepathically, but is visually upset. *"This is a direct threat."* He stands. "How could they get by undetected?"

"There's no reason to overreact and cause alarm," states Sahn. *"We think there might be a change in the hole. It might have been an accident."*

Victor leans on the table with his fists. *"Accident or not, they are in violation of the treaty."*

"He's right. The Simerin got past our ships unnoticed and without permission," argues AmanKi. *"These are acts of aggression."*

"This has happened before, and it was quietly resolved. There's nothing on this planet that they don't already have," replied El, a Monahdah from Los Alamos.

"Everything except the planet itself and control of this sector! That's what they've always wanted." Victor paces to where AmanKi sits. *"And I don't call a battle that lasted two Earth moons a quiet resolution. My grandfather was killed. Several of our space crafts escaped and crash landed bringing attention to us and losing a Mon tablet that still hasn't been retrieved."*

"Minniedah is passionate about this planet." AmanKi said apologetically to their guest. *"When the others arrive we'll make a plan."*

"That's two moons from now," says Victor. *"We should push them out while we have the chance. Before it's too late."*

"We will reason with them first, if possible," says El.

"Diplomacy has never come first with Simerin," said Sahn.

"It does with us. Otherwise we would be like them," commands AmanKi.

AmanKi places his hand on Victor's shoulder. "You have something you would like to tell us?"

Victor takes a sip of his tea. He was going to tell them the important news about Anah. It was on his list of things to discuss, but something told him that it wasn't the right time. "Not at this time."

He walks outside and the light of the full moon leads him down the path to his room. A flash across the sky from the New Mexico band departing in their pods reminds him of his departure and how much he wishes to smooth things out with Anah before he leaves. He understands her feelings of distrust and will give her the space she needs to sort out all of the news about her father and himself. He also knows that she knew there was something very different about herself—Something that she couldn't explain until now.

AmanKi wants Victor to resume his training like they had planned. He would have to leave with the next ship, and his earliest return to Earth would be in two hundred and seventy-six Earth moons. He was eager to leave since being a Keeper is what he was born and bred to do. He's proud and honored to be a part of that tradition. He didn't mate while on Earth. No one met his requirements in order to bear him the perfect son whom he would take with him twelve Earth moons after conception. This plan changed when he met Anah. It's a wonder that she exists. It's something that hasn't happened in his father's lifetime or even his grandfather's grandfather. A flower has bloomed. Anah's existence is a Monahdah miracle.

He takes something off his bookshelf that's flat and clear. He touches it, and it lights up revealing a written manuscript in foreign symbols. He reads the Monahdah text about the Goddess Nahanah. She represents a girl that is born every two thousand years to the Monahdah. She's born before a great war and will give birth to a powerful Monahdah Keeper who will bring balance to the universe.

He knew he could have conceived a child with her already. Her egg was ready to be fertilized yesterday. The chemistry with her isn't anything like he's experienced. His sense of physical control has been difficult. It must be because she is also Monahdah. He wonders how she has gone unnoticed until now. Thankfully she was wearing the Mon ring the evening he decided to go out and mingle with the locals.

His father calls for Victor to join him in the main house. Tonight they will share a meal together. AmanKi has prepared a mixture of rice, herbs and tomatoes with pine nuts that the New Mexico band brought as a gift.

"*Lamu Nahma, Meirlies,*" Victor says.

"MiLamu Nahma," says his father.

Victor waits for his father to take a bite of his food, and a sip of the drink, as is the custom, before he begins.

AmanKi spreads his cloth napkin over his lap. *"There was something you withheld from the group today. You've been keeping a secret."*

Victor looks down at his food ashamed that he must lie. *"I'm not sure what you mean."*

"Have you conceived yet?" asks AmanKi.

"No."

"I can't make you leave with the ship. That's not our way." AmanKi sips from his glass. *"I'm sorry for coming across contrary to that way."*

"You were a Keeper. It will be an honor to continue that tradition. Especially now that Simerin have rescinded the treaty, it will be my duty."

"Tell me about Anah."

"I like her very much."

"I observed you together at the beehives. I don't know how this could be possible, but she can hear you. She has telepathy, doesn't she?"

"Yes."

"I've yet to meet adamah with this quality, but I have heard of it. Some adamah are more evolved, particularly with this generation."

Victor takes a sip. *"Yes, I agree."*

"She would make a good mate, then."

Victor smiles and continues his meal. He's not ready to reveal the entire truth about Anah. He wants to make amends with her first.

AmanKi raises his glass. "To Anah." They clink their glasses.

A Storm Is Coming

I'm standing at my window, unable to look away from the radiance of the moonlight as I think about who or what I am. Why was I supposed to be a big secret? Why was I left behind? I don't know what my father's alien motives are. I'm not going to be a victim like Mom. She was manipulated, even had her memory and her emotions tampered with. Taking care of a baby, like my mother did at my age, is not something I have in mind. The facts are my father is an alien, and he abandoned us. Therefore, he and Victor can't be trusted. This could be some kind of plot to take over Earth, and here I am falling into its trap. I can easily go back to my normal life before I found out that I wasn't exactly human. I'll go to college and be a normal college student. Study science and put my math skills to use. I could study with the top physicists in the country, maybe even the world. Most of all, I just want everything to be normal!

A movement outside, in the trees on the side of the house, diverts my attention. I've noticed my vision has dramatically improved, and I can see exceptionally well in the dark. With the moonlight it's practically like daylight to my eyes. There it is again! Fifteen yards from the house an object moved from one tree and to another. What is it? A deer? A Bear? We've had bear in our yard before when I left the trash cans out. I better go make sure the cans have been put away.

The cans are still outside by the end of the driveway. Lightning flashes in the distance, and a sudden wind gust disturbs the stillness. I grab the trash cans and put them in the garage. Something stirs behind me—a shuffle, a swoosh. I spin around, but nothing is there. I hurry back into the house and back to my room. I have to shield my eyes from my ring on my bedside table. It's glowing bright red as if it's plugged into an electrical current. The only time I've seen it shine bright was when Victor was around, but this is a whole new level. My heart pounds, and blood rushes throughout the network of my veins. My lungs send oxygen to my heart. What's happening? Why do I involuntarily feel so alert?

"Mom!"

"Yeah? What's wrong?" Mom's reading her book on the couch.

I panicked and called out for Mom. I try to reverse my alarming tone and answer in a relaxed state. "Oh, nothing. You're so quiet. I wanted to make sure you were still here."

"Where else would I be?"

"I don't know. Maybe you had to go to work."

"It's 9:30. I would tell you if I were to leave, like I normally do."

I look out the kitchen window. Nothing looks out of the ordinary. The moon casts shadows of the trees, and the wind blows them all around. "I think it's gonna storm." A cloud passes over the moon and everything darkens. Lightning flashes and thunder rumbles in the distance. "We could use the rain," says Mom turning the page of her new book.

I go back to my room and look at the ring that's back to normal brightness. Maybe it senses atmospheric pressure, and the weather has an affect on it somehow.

My mind wanders to the night I met Victor when I first discovered this ring. Perhaps we wouldn't have met if I didn't wear Mom's leather jacket. Then my life would be as if I didn't know anything about my father or Victor. Mom did say that I was to find it when I was ready. Maybe I'm just not ready.

Lightning flashes and lights up my room. I open the drawer to my bedside table and put the ring in a small jewelry box to safely stow it away. Out of my sight, and hopefully out of my mind. I know I can't go back in time and unmeet Victor, but maybe putting the ring away will make it easier.

A loud crack of thunder and lighting flashes outside my bedroom window revealing a silhouette of someone standing not far from my room, but I wake up. It was only a dream. I drifted into sleep long enough to have a disturbing dream. I was running through the woods, afraid for my life. I was captured by aliens who were ugly and smelly. I couldn't understand their language, but somehow I could understand what they were thinking through the use of telepathy. They were going to mate with me in order to start a superior race. They thought that somehow it would give them control of all the planets, including Earth. They argued over a plan to kill me. The one who seemed to be in command said they would use me to negotiate and kill me afterward. I tried to scream for help, but no sound came out of my mouth.

Space Time

"Zeit ist eine Illusion." —Albert Einstein

Mr. Rotter writes Einstein's theory of special relativity on the blackboard with the equation, $E=mc^2$

This actually sparks conversation in the class. It goes against common sense for most of the students. If you accept the idea that time is an illusion since it's relative to space and the observer, it's easier to grasp. He theorizes that time is like a series of events through the spacetime continuum, like a pile of snapshots put together. We discuss the theories of space travel and if one could change the past in order to alter the future or change the future to alter the past. I believe that actually nothing would be altered; only a new branch of time would begin, like a tree growing another branch. Time is like a spider spinning her web.

The bell rings for lunch. "It's *time* for lunch," Mr. Rotter jokes. "Oh and take one of these permission slips with you, and please return it to me tomorrow with a parent or your guardian's signature. We're going on a field trip to Los Alamos." I grab a permission slip on my way out— interesting coincidence.

Los Alamos

Twenty of us happily disembark from the bus. The drive felt life threatening going up the plateau. Mr. Rotter talked the entire time and kept his eyes more on us than the curvy road.

"Your Mom let you keep the ring?" says Sophia sitting next to me. I wanted to test fate again and wear it on this field trip to Los Alamos.

"Yeah, she gave it to me."

"What is that stone? And why does it glimmer like that?"

I have to lie, of course. "It's manmade. It glimmers because it senses fluctuation in temperature."

An elderly man with clear blue eyes and thick gray hair greets us. He's a walking encyclopedia regarding nuclear weapons and the top secret Manhattan Project. This black project was the first of its kind and was so closely guarded that Vice President Truman didn't know about it until after he became president. After his lecture on the first atomic bomb and how it ended a war but started a cold war with Russia, he allows us to wander the museum freely.

"Please, everyone meet me back at the bus in twenty minutes," instructs Mr. Rotter.

I stare at the atomic bomb photos of the first detonation at the Trinity site in Alamagordo. Science is a double-edged sword. It's used to destroy mankind as well as advance it. As the photos come to life for me, they serve as a reminder of the mass destructive power that is not for the advancement of mankind.

"Time to get back to the bus, Anah," says Sophia.

"K, I'll be there in a sec... have to use the bathroom."

A janitor mops the floor in the girls' bathroom, so I have to wait. "Don't slip now and break your pretty little neck," he says as he walks by. He stops short and backs up a step. He looks down and grabs a hold of my hand. I catch my breath and snatch back my hand. "What are you doing?!"

"That...that stone!"

He's seen this stone before! "What about it?"

"Where did you get it?"

"Why are you so interested?"

His old, tired, gray eyes stare into mine. "Who are you?" I ask. He quickly turns away. "Wait! Do you know my father?" He dashes out the bathroom door, leaving behind his mop and bucket.

Sophia enters the bathroom. "Are you coming? We're all waiting for you on the bus."

"Yeah, I'm coming."

Sophia eyes the old man storming out. "Are you okay, Anah?"

"Yeah."

The bus ride home is quiet. Everyone is tired of talking and listening to someone talking. Mr. Rotter wants to give us space to contemplate our visit. Several students put on their headphones. I replay my strange encounter in the bathroom. I didn't sense that I was in danger from this man. In fact, it was quite the opposite. He felt afraid. I sensed fear emanating from his entire being.

We arrive back at school early, so Mr. Rotter tells us to have study hall and write an essay about the pros and cons of nuclear energy.

While writing my essay I look up at Sophia who's getting ready to ask me if I want to go to the movies. "Do you and Victor want to go see a movie with Tim and me this weekend?"

"I don't think that would be a good idea."

"Why not? Didn't you guys have fun with us?"

"Of course I did." I tap my pencil too hard and break the tip. "It's just... I decided to end things with Victor."

"That explains why you've been acting so strange. You guys seemed so great together."

"Nothing is ever what it seems."

"Then what is it?"

I search for a reason to explain my predicament. "He hasn't been honest with me."

"Did you tell him yet? Does he know you don't want to see him anymore?"

"Yeah, he knows." I write my name with my broken pencil tip and put today's date on my paper. Sophia's face turns to stone.

"What's the matter?" The chair slides out next to me. I look up, and Victor stands right next me!

Sophia makes an excuse to leave and joins Tim at the other table. My stomach shoots out butterflies when Victor sits next to me. "Victor, what are you doing here? You can't just waltz in here without permission."

"I just did. They really should do something about that. Anyone could waltz right in." He looks at me with those aqua eyes that can melt an ice-cold heart. "Anah, I know you don't want to continue seeing me, and I understand, but we really need to talk."

"Not right now, Victor. Not here."

"Come with me, then."

"Right now?"

"Yes. Come with me, right now."

"I can't just leave school."

"Yes, you can." He puts his warm hand on my knee. "Tell them you are unwell." I try to resist, but I feel myself softening. I know he's transferring positive energy onto me. He smiles from the corner of his mouth. Damn, how does he do that? I guess the same way that I made my mom's date sick some years ago. Anyway, I don't want to send mixed signals, but I agree to go.

Run Away

We're walking toward Victor's Oldsmobile, and my heart beats with anticipation. It's a little exhilarating to break the rules. I don't like to stir things up or draw attention to myself, so leaving school seems very rebellious.

Before he can come around to open the door and call me his queen, I put my hand on the car door handle. "I got it, Victor."

He puts his hand on top of mine, and I can't help notice the warm tingles his hand creates. He stares at me for a moment, and I cloud my thoughts so he can't read them. I've gotten the hang of this ability. It's similar to walking through thick fog, but it's in the mind. It creates static, like you're between radio signals.

I open the door and quickly hop in. I remind myself that I have no intention of prolonging this and making it harder for the both of us.

I see him, peripherally, glancing over at me. I know I could listen to his thoughts, but that will only let him in my head. I'm not about to do that. I don't like how vulnerable I feel when I'm in his presence, but I'm strong and have confidence that I can end our budding relationship. However thrilling it is to be around Victor, I don't want to be a part of an alien conspiracy. I just want normalcy.

I stare out the window and realize we're at the Aspen Vista trailhead. It's fall, and the aspens are at their peak color. The many shades of yellow, gold, even pink and orange glisten in the sun against the clear, blue sky. I hate to admit this, but he's picked a perfectly romantic breakup spot. He walks around to my side of the car and opens the door. I get out, stuff my hands into my coat pockets and walk slightly behind him. But our footsteps and our breath sound together as we hike up the trail. I keep the static in my heart and the fog in my mind.

We approach a creek, and we both stop to gaze at the slow current of the water. The water is at its lowest level, after the summer monsoons have gone, and before the winter snow. It's my favorite time to sit by the creek and under a canopy of yellow and gold aspen trees. The water gently flows around rocks and fallen leaves instead of pushing and rushing.

"I like it, as well," says Victor.

Shit. I let him in. "Victor, I...we..." Victor picks up a gold leaf. "I don't want to see you anymore. I thought I made that clear last night."

"I know," he says, twirling the stem of the leaf between his fingers. "And I know why."

"You and your people, whatever you are, are like rapists. My mother told me about my father, that is, everything she could remember because you have some way of erasing memories. I don't want to end up like her." He lets go of the leaf, and it falls into the creek, captured in the slow current.

"I understand," he says picking up another autumn leaf.

"So then there's no point in dragging this out between us. Don't worry. I'm not going to tell anyone about you."

"That would be foolish because it would only bring possible harm to you, which is what I don't want. I would never harm you,

Anah." He looks away from the creek and stares into me. He actually looks hurt, and I feel a pang of guilt in my heart. I can feel my knees buckle. He's doing it. He's using whatever power he has to weaken me.

"It's not just me, you know," he says looking back down at the creek. He sits down, but I remain standing and cross my arms.

"What's that supposed to mean?" I snap.

"You have just as much 'power' over me." He picks up a stick this time. "I feel the same way when I'm around you, Anah — light-headed, tingly. Your body glistens and has the sweet scent of a rose, but I don't think of it as a weakness the way you do."

I'm thrown off track. "Victor, please take me back to school." I start to walk back to his car. There's no point in having a discussion with him. I've made up my mind, and we'll both have to deal with it.

"Your Father left you because he was trying to protect you."

I quickly turn around. "From what? Aliens like you?"

He stabs the ground with the stick. "Aliens that would stop at nothing to end your life." He walks toward me. "If they knew you were alive they would have killed you already."

For some reason, I run. If someone asked me why right at this moment, I wouldn't have a rational explanation. I don't even know where I'm running to. I just want to escape from all of this. I want to be alone, away from my thoughts, away from someone listening to them, away from him, away from me. The path leads further into the aspen forest. Victor's behind me, so I leave the path and run deeper into the forest, leaping fallen trees and rocks before finally coming to a stop. A raven caws above. A grazing young buck lifts his head. I've lost him. I turn around, but there he stands, eight feet away. I try to dodge him, but he grabs me, and we fall to the ground. The deer prances away.

"Get away from me!" I scream. "I want to be left alone!"

"I told you, I would never hurt you," he says almost out of breath.

He wraps his arms around my body, and I wrestle to escape. My struggle seems futile. I'm pinned underneath him and his incredible strength. Recovering, I realize how deep in the forest we are. No trail to be seen in any direction. I breathe in his intoxicatingly sweet scent and feel the heat pouring off his body. "I would never hurt you," he whispers. A strong whip of wind creates a rain of yellow aspens leave. "If you don't want to see me anymore then I'll stay away. But I don't believe you. How can I believe you when you don't even believe it yourself?"

I'm lost in his eyes and feel a struggle between what I want and what I'm afraid of. What am I afraid of, exactly? Change? Growing up? The unknown?

"Is that what you want, Anah?"

My eyes fill with tears. I'm not afraid of Victor. I'm afraid of what I don't know or understand, mainly, about myself. This is a significant moment. Am I going to take on what life has given me, or walk away and live the life I already know and understand but never fit into?

My hands move around his waist. I feel his biceps relax as he loosens his grip. I reach up and touch his face. He rests his forehead against mine. Then we kiss. It's hungrier and deeper than ever before. We lose control. Like animals, we roll around in a bed of golden leaves, and I'm now on top of him. His hands pull me in tight so that our bodies are pressing against each other. I've never felt so close to anyone before, as if resisting was going against nature. There's a force between us that only seems to get stronger and more out of our control.

"I'm scared, Victor."

"I know."

"I don't want you to take advantage of me and leave me."

"I want to protect you, Anah."

We stop kissing to catch our breath.

"Why am I in danger?"

"Because you were born."

"How's that any different from you or your father?"

"You're special."

"I don't see why."

"You're a female."

"Yeah, the last time I checked. So?"

"Monahdah only have males."

"Hold on. Then how the hell do you have babies? If you don't have females then how can you even…" I realize the answer before I finish my sentence, of course. They breed with the women here on Earth. *"How long have you, the Monahdah, been doing that?"* I ask referring to my last thought.

"Since we created modern man. The missing link theories are false. Monahdah make up that missing gene. Our genesis scientists are the reason you're not still living in trees."

"Why did the Monahdah come here? What was the purpose?"

"We're explorers, scientists… It's just what we do. We create life. We colonize. Our planet was uninhabitable when it was badly damaged in war, so we came to Earth."

"And to procreate."

"Yes, but well before Adamah."

"Adamah?"

"Humans." He props himself up to sit. "Monahdah have been to Earth before Earth was even a planet. Well, it was a planet but not as it is today. This solar system was still unstable, and Earth was more than twice as big before it happened."

"Before what happened?"

"The great collision."

"Ahh… I've heard of this theory or Sumerian myth."

"On the contrary, the Sumerians have recorded history well. Earth was a much larger planet called Tiamat. After the collision, the Earth, or Ki was essentially created and set on her new course. Evidence of this collision has been right in front of astronomers all along."

"The asteroid belt!"

"Precisely!"

My sweat dries on my skin, and I catch a chill. The sun is low in the sky, and I realize it's getting late. He takes my hand and pulls me up off the ground. "Let's get back to the car."

As we walk back to the car, we talk more about the Monahdah and the Mon stone like the one in my ring. We reflect back on what we were thinking when we first met and all the times we could hear each others thoughts, including the time I heard him and his father telepathically communicate, and we have a good laugh. We both feel it. Our relationship is now at another level, and it feels good.

I'm a Mutant

As I remove my coat, I ask, "So, how did I happen, if you can't have females?"

"I don't know. A mutation, I guess."

"Great, I'm a mutant."

He laughs. "A beautiful one." He removes an aspen leaf tangled in my hair. *"There's a Monahdah legend that every two thousand years a female is born before a great war, and peace will be restored by her offspring. She's the Goddess Nahanah."*

"There's many stories like that, though. The most well known, of course, is the Virgin Mary."

"Story or not, they will want to kill you. You are Monahdah, and they want to destroy what they are afraid of."

"I couldn't harm anybody."

"You have awareness that you haven't even begun to tap into, or that you have taught yourself to ignore. If you have a Monahdah child, that child would be a God-man."

"Or God-woman," I give him a playful shove. "Victor, who are *they*, other Monahdah?"

"*Simerin,*" he says with a sharp edge to his voice. *"We used to be one big empire, but when we started to colonize, we became divided. They destroyed our original planet, Mon. We've had many battles over this planet. They have always been envious of us."*

"Why?"

"They dislike anything natural. They have over cloned themselves and are no longer connected to life force."

"And they are jealous of that?"

"They feel threatened by that."

"You've fought with these Simerin?"

"I never have, but I would to protect our colonies and the universe from destruction."

"What would they do if they came to Earth?"

"What they've done to other planets. Invade and kill most of the inhabitants, or make them slaves to their work and science. Strip the planet of all its natural resources."

"But you prevent them, otherwise they would have already?"

"Yes, we are trained to keep peace and to go into battle."

"You mean like a Jedi?"

He laughs. "It's actually quite similar."

I shift my body closer to him. "Victor, were you at my house last night?"

"I should confess. I was concerned for you because I sensed fear."

"Fear?" I place my hand on his.

"I came to the house but didn't want you to know. I didn't want to further agitate you, so I kept my distance."

"So it was you that I saw out my window?"

Victor narrows his eyes, and lines of concern wrinkle between his brows. "I'm sure it wasn't me. What did you see exactly?"

"I didn't see anything directly, only peripherally. It might have been an animal, like a deer or something."

"What was it? A four legged being or two legged?"

"I don't know. My ring glowed really bright. Mom said that my father wanted her to be very careful. I'm surprised that she even let me go to school."

"Yes, she has kept you well. If it wasn't for that ring, I may not have noticed you right away."

"I did something that perhaps I shouldn't have done. It was probably reckless of me, but I wore my ring to Los Alamos. Some man freaked out when he saw it. He seemed scared and quickly left the room. He recognized the stone. I'm sure of it."

"He's probably the famous scientist, Allen King."

"But he wasn't a scientist, he was a janitor."

"He's not anything now. He was found dead at his home in Los Alamos today."

"What? But I just saw him."

"His dog barked and barked at the window until the neighbor called the police. They said it looked like a suicide."

"Oh my God!"

"He was fired many years ago and was unable to acquire work because the government slandered him and made him out to look crazy. He talked freely about flying saucers and extra-terrestrial technology. His top secret assignment was to reverse engineer one of our space crafts that crashed not far from here where they obtained a very precious slab of Mon."

"This stone is important to you."

"It's not just a stone. It's condensed cosmic energy, an element that is a hundred percent stable and will never decay. It's how we begin life on other planets. You were definitely putting yourself at risk when you wore your ring."

"Do you think I'm in danger?"

"I don't know. No one knows about you except me, and of course, your father. My father will know soon enough. He's already learned that you have telepathy. That's not enough to cause alarm. Besides, I'll keep very close tabs on you," he says as he intertwines his fingers with mine, "if I have your permission."

"If you behave," I say as I give him a little poke.

"We'll need to take extra precautions, though."

"Like what?"

"I should train you."

"Train me?"

"So you will know how to protect yourself. I already know you can run."

"Are you kidding? You had no problem catching up to me."

"That's because I've been trained since the age of ten. I actually put in extreme effort to catch you, Anah." He looks at me with those sultry eyes, and I feel a little proud. "We'll start training tomorrow." He smiles playfully, leans against me and presses me down into the seat with his weight on top of me.

"You definitely didn't seem to have a problem catching me," I say in a playful tone.

"I thought I lost you." He brushes a lock of my hair to the side. "I knew you were special from the first time I saw you."

"You mean the first time you banged into me."

He kisses me, and we sink into the leather of his front seat.

Soon I'll have to go home and do my homework and live a double life. A life where I'm a normal senior getting ready for college and another where I'm the only female of an alien race whose life might be in jeopardy from Simerin, another alien race.

"Before I forget," Victor gets up and reaches for something in the back of the seat. "This is for you and your mom." He hands me a small, brown paper bag. I pull out a jar of honey. It has a label with a bee in the middle and the name Surya at the top. Light shines through the jar revealing a beautiful golden color.

"This is awesome. Thank you, Victor. Mom will love it!"

He opens the jar and dips his finger in. "Taste."

I taste the honey from his finger. The nectar is so sweet and delicious. Words can't describe it. He sucks the rest of the honey from his finger. "Can you taste the flowers?"

"Yes." I try to hold back tears. I wrap my arms around him. "I'm so sorry Victor. I shouldn't have run."

"I'm sorry, too. I want you to trust me."

"I do."

"So," he gives me a half grin. "Would you like to see me again?"

"I don't know," I snicker. "You aren't very convincing."

He dips his finger in the honey again. "Perhaps you need another taste."

I taste the honey again from his finger, and at the same time he kisses and sucks the honey from my lips, and we become completely absorbed in the sensuality of the kiss.

Dr. Vogel

I breeze through calculus while making a poor attempt to redirect my thoughts. They way heavily on my father. Guilt has replaced what used to be pain. A new sense of clarity has freed me of the anger and hatred I held against him. What a jerk I've been. How was I to know that my Dad was an alien, and I'm the only female of his kind! How was I to know that there's an enemy, alien race with harmful intentions? This anger is so embedded in me that it feels strange to let it go. I'm slowly rising from the deep, dark depths of water to where there's light. I wonder where he is at this very moment and if he can hear my plea for forgiveness.

I clasp my hands together like I'm about to pray. *"This is Anah, your daughter."*

A mysterious sense of strength grows in the pit of my belly. He's kept me a secret, and now I know why. I tell him in my mind that I'm sorry. It feels good to be free of the negative emotions that have paralyzed me for so long. When I look into the mirror my face looks different, softer, and the lines between my brows are gone.

I don't completely grasp the idea that I'm part alien, though, or that my father and my boyfriend are from another planet. Maybe I'll wake up any minute and be somewhat relieved that this is all a dream.

I wonder how this would change the world if the world knew that there are bigger enemies out there, and their biggest danger isn't from other humans or religions but other planets with intelligence far superior to ours.

My phone buzzes in my back pocket with a text from Sophia.

"Did you breakup with Victor? How did it go?"

"We didn't break up. Evryth kul. Or should I say HOT!"

"OMG :o," Sophia texts. "Wanna double date?"

"Maybe. I'll see if Victor's up for it."

"Awesome ☺"

"Mmm. This tea is so delicious with the honey Victor gave us." Mom says as she comes into my room uninvited. She puts a cup on my desk. "Here, I made you some." She sits on the edge of my bed. I look at her expecting one of her talks. The hot tea is usually a precursor to one.

"Thanks."

"The next time you decide to leave school feeling sick, you should let me know. At least answer your phone and my texts."

"You're right. I should have let you know." That way at least she won't call me again in the middle of a make out session with Victor.

"Honey, I know you've been spending time with Victor." She pauses and uncomfortably takes another sip of the tea. Now I know. It's the sex talk. "Are you two becoming intimate?"

"Mom, we have sex-ed at school." I'm not sure why I dread these conversations, but I do. "And I read the books you gave me when I started my period."

"It's not just that, Anah. I don't want to see you get hurt."

She's speaking from her past experience, so I try to be more sensitive. "I appreciate that, Mom, but I can't live my life if I'm gonna be afraid all the time."

"I know. I just know that when you are young hormones can be hard to control. So I would like you to go to Dr. Vogel. He can talk to you about different kinds of birth control. If you and

Victor want to be in a relationship then you both need to be responsible."

I laugh when I remember what Victor told me if I did have a child with a Monahdah, that the child would be like a living god.

"You need to take this seriously, Anah. If you have sex, you can get pregnant."

I want to end the conversation and for her to get out of my room, so I comply. "Okay, I'll go see Dr. Vogel, Mom."

"Good. Thank you for being mature about this."

"Anytime," I mumble and take a sip of the tea.

I've never gone to Dr. Vogel before. I never had a reason to since he's an OB/GYN. I guess I've graduated from well child checks and the occasional immunization shot to women's health checks with breast exams and pap smears. Fun.

"Your appointment is on the first Friday of November at 4:00."

"You already made my appointment?" I snap.

"It was originally supposed to be my appointment, but I switched it so you don't have to wait."

"Great, Mom. Thanks."

"You're welcome. Love you."

She's only doing what responsible parents do. I should be less annoyed. "Love you, too."

Just A Deer

I change into my sweats, wash my face and brush my teeth. I don't usually wear makeup, but I sometimes wear eyeliner. My hazel eyes are one of my best features. Anyway, it feels good to go to bed with clean fresh skin. I walk back down the hall toward my room when I feel a presence and spin around, but no one is there. After I enter my bedroom, I still have the feeling. In the corner of my room stands a dark shadowy figure. Victor steps out into the light.

"Victor!" I gasp. "Are you trying to scare the shit out of me?"

"That was pretty good," he says looking satisfied.

"Yeah, you scared the shit out of me!"

"You could sense my presence without seeing me."

"So, who can't do that?"

"Many can't," he says. "This is the beginning of your training."

"You said we wouldn't start 'til tomorrow."

"I'm a little early," he says glancing at my clock which reads 11:45, and I chuckle.

"This is no laughing matter," says Victor.

"Victor, I'm not starting my training at midnight."

"Let's go for a late night stroll. The moon is almost full." I kiss him on the cheek. "That sounds like a better idea."

I zip up my down coat. It's a clear, cool, fall evening. Next week is Halloween. I used to go trick-or-treating with Sophia in her neighborhood because my closest neighbor is twenty acres away. This reminds me of our annual Halloween dance at school. "You want to go to our school dance next Friday?"

"Okay," he says.

"You don't have to, but most people are going to wear a costume."

"Oh, right. In honor of your autumn custom of Halloween."

"Yeah."

"I'm sure I can come up with something interesting to wear."

"I'm going as a witch since I already have a costume." I'm excited. I never had a date to the Halloween dance before. I reach in his coat pocket and hold his warm hand.

"Don't you get tired?" I curiously ask.

"Not really. That's a human trait and should be a part of your training."

"Not to get tired?"

"I notice that you sleep."

"I lay awake mostly. When I do finally sleep it's interrupted by my dreams."

A quick movement of a shadowy figure dashes into the woods. We simultaneously stop walking. It was so brief that I could have imagined it, but I don't think Victor thinks so. He lets go of my hand. *"Don't move."*

Before I can protest he's gone in the direction of the moving figure. I creep in the direction of the trees about twenty yards behind Victor. I peek around a tree but don't see or hear anything. Suddenly I hear movement, and the sound of struggle. I run in the direction of the sound and peer down at Victor wrestling with a deer. The deer drags Victor a few feet before it escapes and disappears into the woods.

"Victor! Are you crazy?"

He gets up, grabs my arm and walks me briskly away.

"Let's go! It's not safe!"

"Yeah, the deer might come back to get us."

"That wasn't a deer."

"Victor, on this planet it is. That was just a deer."

"I'll explain at the house."

Even though I know Mom took her sleeping pills, I open and close the door as quietly as possible and tiptoe to my room. She would be upset to know I was wandering around outside in the middle of the night. I take off my coat and plop down on the bed. "Okay, what do you think it was then, that deer?"

"A spy."

"The deer was spying on us?"

"He changed into a deer to escape as I tackled him. It might be what you thought you saw the night before."

"How is that even possible?"

"It is."

I grab my head as I try to discern what he's telling me. "You can shape shift into animals?"

"Yes. Well, not always, but it's possible."

"That's crazy. Can you?"

"I'm not there yet."

"Oh." I didn't hide my disappointment.

"Yeah, it's a bit disappointing. Many cultures, like the Native Americans for instance, believe in shape shifting. The Navajo speak about 'skin-walkers.'"

"Will I have this gift?"

"We'll know when you start training."

"Then I want to start now!"

"I think we've had enough excitement for now. I need to talk to my father, and you need to come with me."

"Can't it wait? I don't want to leave in the middle of the night with Mom here all alone. Besides, I want to start training now that I know shape shifting is involved. I hope I can turn into something cool like a bird, maybe even an owl. I love owls." I walk around my room feeling very alive and alert. "Can you choose your animal?"

"Some masters can. It's usually a surprise and feels similar to a dream state when it happens. I believe the animal spirit chooses you," Victor says this as he looks intently out the window. "I'll stay here, and in the morning I'll speak to my father." The clock on my nightstand reads 1:01a.m. Victor keeps a restless watch from my window. The yard and nearby woods are under his constant surveillance. He's also pumped full of adrenaline, and you can see his veins are enlarged since he just wrestled with a deer or in this case, an alien spy.

"Why don't you sit down?" I gesture to a place on the bed beside me. He sits down next to me, and I kneel behind him and wrap my arms around his neck. He's completely tense, and I kiss his neck in an attempt to relax him. It seems to work. He grabs a hold of my arms, stands up and twirls me around playfully, and then we crash land onto the bed.

"Maybe I should try to get some sleep," I say as we snuggle on the bed together. "I'll stay here. You won't have to worry," he says. I lay my head on his chest, and the rhythm of his breathing and the beating of his heart relaxes me. "I'm not worried," I say as I close my eyes and fall asleep.

My sleep is interrupted by nightmares. I'm running through the woods because someone or something is chasing me. I feel a jolt against my back, and I fall to the ground. I wake up kicking and flailing my arms.

"It's okay, Anah." Victor has a strong grip on my arms. "Your consciousness is just active. You're okay."

I come back to reality. "Sorry, Victor. I've been having these dreams. I'm running for my life. They're disturbing."

Victor lies close behind me and puts his arm around me in comfort. I roll over to face him. "Pay attention to your dreams. They could hold important messages, maybe preparing you for something."

"Maybe I have trouble sleeping because I'm not supposed to sleep."

"How many hours do you normally sleep?"

"Four or five hours." I flip my pillow over. "How about you?"

"I do what's more like a nap, but it's meditative."

"You're not really asleep?"

"Yes."

"And you don't get tired?"

"Not when you learn to control the mind."

"What are you thinking about when you're controlling your mind?"

"Nothing. That's the point."

"What about your body? Doesn't it need to rest?"

"Sometimes. I am part human. Monahdah only need one or two hours. Your lengthy sleep state must be special to you. If I were you, I would listen to your dreams. Translate them exactly as they appear. Keep them close to you when you are awake."

My heart recovers to a normal rate, and my muscles relax again.

"Victor, how old are you?" It's funny that I've never asked before, but since he doesn't need to sleep my mind wanders to his mortality.

"I was born in North Africa on June 9th, the *same* year as you."

I sigh with relief. "Oh good! We're the same age. I was expecting you to say something strange, like a hundred years old."

"My father is. He's 110."

"He had you when he was ninety three?"

"In Earth years. Monahdah can breed late in life. Ninety is young."

"He doesn't look a day over thirty."

I take a deep breath. "How long can you live then?"

"My great grandfather's father is alive. His father probably would be also, but he was killed in battle."

"All of your grandfathers are still alive basically."

"Not my father's father. He was killed in battle as well."

"That must have been recent."

"Yes, my father was with him but was too late to prevent it from happening. You're familiar with the Roswell incident."

"Only that a UFO had apparently crashed on a ranch there, and the government covered it up."

"My father took down those crafts. Simerin got past our borders. They refused to leave, so we attacked. My grandfather didn't survive. My father did survive. I wouldn't be here right now otherwise, so I'm very grateful."

"I'm glad you're here, Victor."

He kisses me on the forehead. "Me, too."

The Bird Overhead

"Space and time are modes in which we think, not conditions in which we exist."— Albert Einstein

We're walking along a sandy arroyo that's thirty feet deep. It's the first day of my training, but so far we haven't done anything strenuous or turned into any animals. "Victor, this is a nice nature walk, but shouldn't we run or do something?"

He points to a pleasant spot with a large deposit of sand from previous downpours of countless monsoons. "*Come sit.*" A group of large, healthy piñon trees enclose the area providing shade and privacy. I do as I'm told and sit facing him cross-legged.

"This is really nice."

"Before one physically trains one must mentally train." He closes his eyes for a few breaths and rests his hands on his thighs. *"Everything around you is energy, the same energy that's within you... Now... imagine that there is no you, only energy."*

I close my eyes and try to follow his instruction, but there's so much distraction, like the birds, wind, leaves, and the fly that just landed on my face. I open one eye to peek at Victor, and although he's sitting right before me his mind is somewhere else. *"I'm sorry, Victor,"* I say after several minutes. *"This isn't working."*

He opens his eyes, and he has a soft gaze about him.

"Okay, I'll break it down and try to simplify things. It's best if you don't try."

"If I don't try, then how am I to do it?"

"It's not something you do, only realize and experience."

He puts his hands on my thighs and instructs me to put my hands onto his.

"Now... imagine we are one and the same, not separate," he says. *"Close your eyes and begin to see with your ears without categorizing any sound into a pleasant sound or an annoying sound. You are only a witness, an observer."*

He makes it sound easy, but it's not. I can hear his breathing and mine, and as far as I can tell we are two separate beings. I don't want to disappoint him, so I keep my eyes closed and try to concentrate.

"Your mind is way too active," Victor interrupts my thinking.

"Sorry."

A few minutes later a chirping bird demands my attention. I try hard not to let the bird distract me, but he won't stop chirping. It's making it very difficult for me to concentrate or not concentrate, or whatever I'm supposed to be doing. The bird is louder and in close proximity to where I'm sitting. I fight the urge to open my eyes, but I can no longer resist. Victor looks like he's asleep. I don't want to move and disturb his concentration. The bird continues to chirp on a low branch in the piñon tree to my left. He finally takes flight in my direction and lands on my knee! I catch my breath and make eye contact with this little creature. He hops up my arm all the way to my shoulder. Wow! The bird flies away. I stand up to see where it went, but he's no longer in sight.

My butt is totally numb, and I wonder how long we've been sitting. "Only forty-five minutes," Victor says breaking the long silence.

Victor stands and brushes away sand from his legs. "Did you like the bird?"

"The one that wouldn't be quiet?"

"The same one that landed on you."

"How did you know that? You had your eyes closed the entire time."

"Because I did that."

"Did what? You made the bird fly over to me?"

"I actually did the flying."

"You were sitting right in front of me."

"My body," he corrects. "I connected with the bird's energy and was able to fly the bird and land on you." He smiles and seems very pleased with himself. "That's something I've never been able to do before. Perhaps teaching is a good tool for my own training."

"I'm glad to be of service," I say a little disappointingly.

"Don't worry. It will come when you least expect it."

"But you were able to 'connect,'" I say using my fingers to quote, "without even trying."

"Remember, I started my training at age ten." He holds my hand as we start to walk. "I want you to do this daily at the same time each day."

"Is this something only Monahdah can do?"

"Some Adamah have this power, especially in eastern cultures."

"Jesus walked on water."

"Yes, these so called 'miracles' are normal to us."

I'm excited and disappointed at the same time. Disappointed because I didn't experience the universal energy. Not having success in something, even when trying it for the first time, is a new experience for me, but I'm excited because my mind has never been stimulated in this way before. "What's next?"

"You're wearing running shoes," he says looking down at my feet. "Let's have a race."

"That's okay. We already know who will win."

"Let's get creative. I will start about one hundred yards east, and I'll give you a head start."

"Where are we racing to?"

"To my room."

"You have a big advantage over me since I don't know the terrain as well as you."

"Hence, the head start."

I tighten my laces. "Just tell me when." I'm waiting for Victor to say go, telepathically, since he'll be out of sight and hearing range.

"Anah," I hear loud and clear.

"Yep."

"Tap into the energy around you, like we did while meditating. Then imagine that you are already in my room." There's a moment of silence from all around. Even the birds stop singing. *"Got it?"*

"Sure, yep, whatever. Let's do this!"

A strange thing occurs. My heart begins to beat as fast as if I'm already running. My mind prepares my body by sending out blood and oxygen to my muscles. I visualize touching Victor's door first, winning the race.

"Get ready. Set. Go!"

I blast out into the trees. I know I have to head north and that we are a good twenty-minute walk from his house, which is almost a mile away. I visualize myself standing in front of Victor's room as I swiftly jump over felled trees and logs. There's no path before me as I sweep through brush and momentarily lose my focus as something sharp scrapes my arm. Despite my now stinging arm, I refocus until I come to a strange muddy, marshy area. I find it odd that it exists here on top of this mesa, which is very dry and arid.

"Damn." I'll have to go around. This will cost me a lot of time. I hang a right since it appears to have a clearer path. I'm breathing hard, and I have to stop to catch my breath.

"Stay relaxed. Stay focused," I hear Victor repeat in my mind.

I'm surprised at how lightly my feet touch the ground when I return my attention. It's an amazing sensation. I see a clearing about fifty yards ahead. As I blast out into the clearing I peripherally see Victor on my right. We're almost exactly tied. His house is in full view directly ahead of us, no more than a hundred yards.

Running neck and neck our legs cut through the wild grasses. I don't think I can run any faster. Victor is now ahead of me. My feet feel heavy again, and I'm straining with intense effort.

"Don't strain! Refocus," he demands.

I return to my vision of touching the door first and ignore Victor running even closer to my right, which is not easy since I can hear his feet touch the ground faster than my own.

His door is only twenty yards away. I'm so focused I forget momentarily about Victor and the race. I experience something that's beyond comprehension. For less than a second it feels as if I'm under water. I hear a loud pop before I touch the door to Victor's room. I have no idea what just happened, but I reached the door first. I won!

Clapping interrupts the strange experience going on in my mind as I recover my breath. Victor laughs to my right, and AmanKi is clapping to my left.

"Let me know when the next race is," his father remarks while clapping.

I rest my hands on my knees to catch my breath.

Victor grins ear to ear and finds whatever just happened very amusing.

"What's so funny?" I manage to ask through my breath and pounding heart.

"I'm just excited," he says. "You were able to come up from behind. That was pretty amazing, Anah."

I look down at my stinging arm that has a deep cut seeping with blood.

"You two," says Victor's father in a serious voice, "come with me."

I feel like we did something wrong, and we're about to be grounded.

"Wait here, Anah. I'll be right back," Victor instructs.

"That won't be necessary. She will join us," says his father. *"Anah, that cut on your arm needs attention."* He communicates with me telepathically, and I take a nervous gulp. There's no pretending this time.

We enter into a huge room with large windows and an excellent panoramic view of the sunset. Wooden beams support the pitched roof, and a stone fireplace is at one end of the room surrounded by antique-looking chairs, sofas and tables. A modern kitchen is at the opposite end. A long table that sits at least thirty people stands in front of glass doors that open to a patio.

Victor's father pours us a glass of water with sprigs of mint leaves. Then he dips a white cloth into the water and dabs the cut on my arm.

"Okay," he says while soaking up the blood on my arm.

"Yes, Meirlies?" Victor says innocently.

"What are you up to?"

"Just a bit of fun."

Victor's father looks down at my arm. *"There, much better."*

I observe his height and strength and remember he's over a hundred years old. I take an awkward sip of my water. He stares down at me, and I'm unable to meet his eyes. "Where did you learn to do that?"

"Do what?" I know that he's referring to how I manipulated spacetime, while racing Victor, but I play dumb.

"No more games." He looks at Victor. *"No more lies."*

I nervously play with my glass and say, *"I'm not sure how it happened. It just did."*

"Who are you, and where are you from?" His deep blue eyes glare into me.

"I'm Anah Weis."

"Anah, I'm sorry. Let me explain." Victor attempts to rescue me. "Meirlies, Anah is one of us."

AmanKi's eyes shift back to me, and he takes a long, hard look. He walks away after an awkward pause and reaches for something above the fireplace on the mantel. It's a pyramid shaped Mon. "Do you know what this is?" he says as he gives me the pyramid to hold. The red and orange lava colors glow and swirl around much brighter where my hands are in contact. A tingling sensation travels up my arms. I don't understand what's happening, so I set the pyramid stone on the table and the stone goes back to its original condition. *"It's okay."* He places a finger on the stone to demonstrate. The light and energy of the stone swirls at the place where he touches it. "It has concentrated astral energy, and it's attracted to like energy. I asked you to hold it because I wanted to see for myself. I know Victor was telling the truth, but that staggering truth is now confirmed."

"Yes, Victor showed me his Mon. I have the same stone at home in my room. It's in a ring that my father gave me."

"Who is your father?"

"I don't know. We've… or I have never met him."

"She recently learned, Meirlies, that she's Monahdah," Victor adds.

"Then I am impressed. Already you have an understanding of other dimensions."

"Not really. I just concentrated on the outcome I wanted."

"It's a remarkable skill to have, especially for an untrained Monahdah."

"It's not something I've done before."

"I want to train Anah," Victor interjects. *"She has a lot of catching up to do, and mind-body development. I don't think it's too late."*

"Why do I sense urgency in you?"

"Must you ask?"

"You feel she's in danger."

"I know she is. She has been watched. Someone knows she is here."

"Yet she is unharmed." Victor's father sits on one of the antique looking chairs. *"If Simerin had any notion of her existence, they would have killed her already or at least tried."*

He turns to look at me. *"Have you been threatened in anyway?"*

"Only scared. I've seen someone at my house, and the other night Victor almost captured whoever or whatever it was, but he shape-shifted and escaped."

Meirlies turns to his son. *"This explains your absence last night?"*

"Yes, I should have told you."

"You are still Minniedah, after all."

"I'm sorry. I do know better."

I realize that Victor is a teenager getting reprimanded by his father. Even though he's an advanced being from another planet, he's not immune to a parent's discipline. My discomfort in the moment compels me to speak on Victor's behalf. "He wanted to go to you right away, but I asked him to stay because I didn't want to leave my mother alone at the house."

"I understand." He smiles at my effort.

Bringing up Mom reminds me that I probably should be heading home. *"Victor, I should be going."*

"Anah, you're most welcome to stay with us," says Victor's father.

"That's very kind of you, sir, but I should get home before my mother worries. I'm still Minniedah, after all."

Victor and his father laugh.

I'm not sure what I said wrong. *"What's so funny?"*

"That means, 'child of mine'," Victor explains.

I giggle with some embarrassment. "I thought it meant teenager. Should I call you Meirlies?"

"Meirlies means father. You may call me AmanKi, or Eamon."

"Okay... Eamon. Thank you for everything."

He looks at me like he's witnessing a miracle. "You're welcome." He places his hand on my shoulder. "Look," he says pointing to my arm. "All better." My arm has completely healed without any marks or sign of injury.

What About The Legend

AmanKi replaces the Mon pyramid on the mantel. *"She really has no idea who her father is."*

Victor adds another log to the hot coals. *"No... but I do."*

"As do I."

"How, may I ask?"

AmanKi nods at the cloth laying on the coffee table that was used to clean Anah's wound on her arm. Victor picks it up and stares at the blood stain on the cloth. *"He has done well keeping her, without anyone finding out, until now."*

"As have you." AmanKi looks at Victor with a raised brow.

"I was afraid to jeopardize her safety."

AmanKi sits, and Victor sits across from him. *"I would have done the same thing. It's obviously what he wanted. Have you told her about her father?"*

"Not yet," Victor leans forward and rests his forearms on his thighs. *"She should live with us. This is her family now, and Anah will be safe."*

"She has gone unnoticed by us for one Earth year, not to mention her whole life thus far. Perhaps it is better to allow things to remain as they are. It will draw attention if she lives here with us."

Victor tossed the cloth back on the coffee table. *"Then I am unable to keep her safe. If she's here, she will train faster. We can create a ruse that she is my wife. Many Monahdah live an earthly life with a human wife. It will seem no different."*

"It will seem obvious. She is not human. She will continue her earthly life accordingly, or else we shall put her life at risk."

Victor stands, and walks close to the fireplace, staring into the flame. *"What about the legend? Shouldn't we put that into consideration?"*

"That's exactly what I'm putting into consideration."

This Reality

Tonight is the dance, and I'm digging around in the Halloween box looking for my witch costume. I've been training all week, and I look forward to switching back to my other life at school. Victor takes this training business seriously, so I'm hoping tonight he'll lighten up and go back to being my boyfriend instead of my trainer teaching me about the cosmos and alternate realities. Tonight I want to focus on this reality and spend quality time with friends.

I look at myself in the mirror unsatisfied with my costume on. I need to accessorize, so I rummage around my room. I find an old, pentagon choker in my dresser drawer and cool spider-hose. I slip on some black high heels, and line my eyes dramatically with black eyeliner and mascara. For my lips I use red lipstick that I borrowed from Mom. Then the perfect final touch— my ring.

Mom chats away with Victor in the kitchen. Of course, he's early. She's making a lot of commotion and says something about finding the camera. I put on my pointy hat and leave my room to see what the fuss is about.

"What!" Victor looks like he just came off a movie set. He's disguised as a werewolf and looks amazingly real. His shirt is torn, and he's added chest and facial hair to match his own. His pants are torn below the knees with added leg hair, and he wears long claws on his hands and feet. He looks like a human wolf.

"You're going to scare the shit out of people."

"Isn't that the idea?"

"Okay. Stand right here." Mom gets the camera ready. We pose in front of the fireplace. Victor puts his claws on my shoulder and pretends he's going to eat me. I place my foot on his thigh to show off my cool spider-hose.

"Say cheese!" The camera flashes.

"You look amazing, Victor!"

"So do you. Things might get a little weird tonight," he says, and I blush and quietly chuckle.

"Have fun," Mom says while snapping more photos. "Victor, please have her home by midnight. It's not safe to be driving around with all the parties and drunk drivers."

"Of course. She's in good hands," he says with his usual politeness.

No One Knows I'm Here

The event club at school has done an awesome job transforming the gym for Halloween. The florescent lights create a glowing, spooky affect. Tables are set up with battery-operated candles and flickering skulls. Tim's father got us the DJ who's playing some weird Halloween version of a B52's song. And of course, what's a school dance without a table loaded with cookies and punch.

I pour punch into my cup, and Victor says, *"I don't think you should be wearing your ring."*

"Why didn't you say something earlier?" I sip my punch. "People here will think it's just part of the costume. It's just a ring, Victor."

"It's not just a ring, and you know that. Someone might notice."

"Anah!" Sophia calls out from behind me. She's wearing a red, sparkly leotard that shows off her figure with red, high heels. The horns on her head, and the trident reveal what she's dressed as. "Holy crap! Stay away from me, you vicious beast." She pokes Victor with her trident.

"The devil is much prettier than I thought," says Victor.

"I like your costume, Sophia," I say.

"Wow, Anah, you look pretty amazing in black. Tim and I are over there." She points to a table at the back of the room. "It's way too loud up here by the dance floor," she yells.

Victor grabs a hand full of cookies and continues his argument. *"It will draw unnecessary attention."*

"What's more obvious? My ring? Or you not communicating like a human? I want to relax and have fun tonight. Can you please act normal?"

"I'm communicating in a loud room, and I'm not acting any differently. I think you're the one who needs to relax."

I'm shocked. He's never talked to me like this before. I realize that Victor and I are having our first fight. Perhaps it's his wolf costume bringing out his alter ego.

"Or your witch costume bringing out yours." He bites into a cookie.

"Touché." I take a hold of his hand, and we casually stroll over to the table. He lays a bunch of cookies down.

Tim wears a black shiny suite. "Hey man. How's it going? Nice costume."

"What are you supposed to be, Tim?" I ask.

Tim picks up a mask on the table and puts it over his head. He turns into an alien with large iridescent eyes. The irony makes me laugh.

Some song by Deadmau5 comes on, and Sophia wants to dance. We hit the empty dance floor and dance like we don't care. One by one the dance floor becomes packed, and the dJ doesn't let us down as he plays popular hits. Tim, Sophia, Victor and I let it all out. Uninhibited, we move our bodies freely. Then I experience something peculiar. I wonder if the punch is laced. The sound of the music sounds far away, like it's in the background miles away. I hear a bell ring, like the sound of crystal. The feeling is overwhelmingly unfamiliar. What the hell is happening? Am I entering into another dimension? Am I dying?

"Victor?" I nervously call out to him. *"What's happening to me?"*

"Relax, Anah, it's okay. You're experiencing energy from its source. You're integrating." His voice reassures me. "Just go with it."

Everyone in the room is now reflecting light, including Sophia and Tim. The light surrounds them, encasing them in a glowing array of colors. Sophia's lips are moving, but I have no idea what she's saying because all sound is diverted from my ears, like I'm inside a bowl. Wrapped together in this illumination of color, there's a lot of movement happening at different intervals and speeds— the dancers, people walking by, or just sitting, watching, listening, yet I'm experiencing it as if everything is occurring at once. Inside this bowl, time is not a dimension that exists. There's no beginning and no end. As soon as I wonder how long this experience will last, it dissipates. The curtain closes. The sound of the music returns, and I'm left with an intense sense of euphoria.

Victor has a big congratulatory smile. He takes ahold of my hand. *"How was it?"* Words can't describe what just happened without it taking away from the ecstasy of the experience, so I don't put it into words.

Victor looks down at my hand because my ring reflects brightly into his eyes. I've never seen it glow this bright, except that night when I saw something lurking outside my window. I pick up nervous tension from him. He anxiously scans the room. Someone standing in the back corner grabs our attention. "Who's that?" The hooded figure quickly turns and walks out through the gym doors.

"I have no idea."

"Wait right here," Victor commands.

There he goes again telling me to stay out of the way. I follow him anyway and catch a glimpse of him pursuing the hooded figure through a back exit door. "What the hell?" I pick up my pace the best I can in high heels. When I open the door a blast of cold wind hits me in the face. I follow Victor and pass some Goth-looking kids sneaking a smoke. When I bend down to remove my heals, I hear Victor's voice around the corner at the back of the school. "Who are you?" Victor says in a demanding tone that frightens me.

"Remove your hands!" says the stranger.

I turn the corner with caution. The last time he had a confrontation, he wrestled with a deer. This time it's a boy, about the same age as Victor, pinned against the wall. Victor has tremendous strength, and I'm afraid he might break the boy's collarbone. However, the boy is built like a man, and I'm not sure if I should be more concerned for Victor. He's over six feet tall, and his large arm muscles are defined under his thick, black hoody. He jabs his knee into Victor's stomach, trying to break free. Victor attacks back with a head punch. Blood sprays out of the boy's nose.

"Stop!" I hear myself scream.

"Anah, go back inside."

"You're not the boss of her!" says the boy telepathically.

I'm stunned and confused. *"How is this boy communicating like us?"* I grab Victor's arm. "Victor! Both of you! Stop!"

They step away from one another, and they are both breathing hard. The three of us stare at each-other until Victor breaks the silence. "Your imposition has come to an end."

"Let's go inside and discuss this," I say shivering, "in a comfortable setting."

"Not until he reveals who he is and what he's doing here!"

The boy looks at me. "I'm her dahman."

"What? What the hell's that?" I ask annoyed that we're still outside.

"Bullshit. She doesn't need your protection. Who sent you?" Victor presses him firmly against the wall.

"She does need my protection with the likes of you!"

Victor returns the comment with a quick punch to his bloody nose, and I hear a bone crunch. The boy jabs his elbow into Victor's neck, and he groans in pain.

"That's enough!" I say stepping between them. "What do you mean, 'my dahman'?"

Victor points over my shoulder saying, "Go back and tell whoever sent you that she doesn't need you."

It's a little annoying to see an advanced being with such an ego, and I remind myself that he is part human. "Victor, he's obviously not here to harm me. You need to cool it. Now, I'll ask again, what the hell does dahman mean?"

Victor takes a hold of the boy's shirt with his fist. "Bodyguard, or protector, but he hasn't answered any questions yet."

The boy knocks Victor's arm away then wipes the blood from his nose. "I came on my own. No one knows I'm here."

I take a step closer. "It was you, wasn't it, outside my window a few nights ago?"

"Yes." The boy uses his hoody to wipe blood dripping from his nose.

I cross my arms. "Why are you sneaking around and spying on me?"

He removes his hood. He looks down at the ring on my hand and then directly into my eyes. There's something strange yet comforting and familiar while I'm caught in his gaze. "You're my Anah," he finally says.

I narrow my eyes at him and nervously expect Victor to throw another punch, but he actually looks apologetic. I take a nervous step back. "What do you mean exactly?"

"ShanahMi," Victor says in Monahdah. He puts his hand on the boy's shoulder. *"Let us go to my home and fix the injury I inflicted upon you,"* Victor says, as I translate the meaning, but I'm fazed. First, Victor wants to bash his head in, and now he wants to help him.

"Please tell me what's going on!"

"Anah is sister. That is, your name in a way, means sister," explains Victor. "Anah, say hello to your brother."

Through his bloody teeth he smiles. "Call me Yemo."

He Marked You

My brother, Yemo, sits on Victor's armchair. His nose has stopped bleeding, but it's misshapen and obviously broken. "Shouldn't we take him to the hospital?"

Victor goes over to him and cups his hands over Yemo's nose. "Ready?" Yemo closes his eyes. I look the other way. Yemo says something loud and indecipherable and I hear something snap.

Victor hands him the Mon stone and says, "Your father doesn't know you're here?"

Yemo places the stone on his nose. "I disobeyed orders and came on my own. He's aware of my absence by now."

Questions form as the shock wears off. "Do we have the same father?"

Yemo moves the Mon to the other side of his nose. "And Mother."

How can that be? Did Mom keep this from me? Her memory was tampered with, so maybe she doesn't remember. "My mom would have mentioned the fact that I have a brother."

"I was taken soon after birth. You were born about fifteen minutes after me."

I feel light headed and need to sit down. I breathe deeply to avoid passing out. "We're twins, you're telling me?"

"Is that the word for it?"

"My... our... mother doesn't know about you?"

"She forgets. I don't think she ought to know." I sense emotional pain coming from him.

"But you want to meet her. That's really why you came?"

"I discovered recently that I have an Anah, a family, and yes, I want to meet my primmonKi."

I look at Victor for translation help. It means, "Mother. Actual translation is female from Earth." He turns his attention back to Yemo. "How did you learn this?"

"I was in training when Meirlies," he looks at me, "that means, 'Father.' He was listening to you, and I heard it as well."

My eyes are open wide with fascination. "What did you hear?"

"You were very upset and angry. You wanted to meet him."

"Wow. You heard that from space?"

"Yeah. We recently arrived at the nearest station."

"Arrived from where?"

"NeuMonah. It's where we spend most our time when we're not breeding or traveling between colonies."

"That's where these comes from?" I gesture to the Mon stone on his face.

He takes the stone off of his nose and looks at it. "These come from Mon. I've never been there. Since we don't live there anymore our life span has diminished. Much of Mon has been mined and what's left lies deep within the planet. Planet Mon will one day be restored."

"I know about some of this from Victor. And now Monahdah come to Earth to breed." It felt a little gross to say that out loud.

"You should ask your boyfriend that," he says sarcastically with a silly grin.

"Do you want another bloody nose?" I ask.

Victor removes the rest of his werewolf costume that didn't come off during his fight with Yemo. "I can tell you two are related."

"So is that when you first learned about me? When our father channeled me?" I ask Yemo.

"Yes. He told me that he was keeping your identity hidden, and that I must do the same."

"MinnEnki will deal with you when he arrives." Victor takes back the Mon stone and places it on his neck where Yemo jabbed his elbow. "In the meantime you can stay here."

"He will be too busy dealing with you to worry about me," says Yemo.

"What's MinnEnki mean?" I ask.

"That's your father's name," says Victor.

I narrow my eyes at him. "You know my father?"

"I've been assigned to train under him," Victor admits, "just recently."

"How the hell do you know he's my father?"

"He marked you, don't you know?" Yemo takes back the Mon in his playful spar with Victor and puts it back on his nose.

I look at Victor and cross my arms waiting for an explanation. "When we kissed, our first kiss, I marked you. I did it out of habit. It usually happens involuntary."

"What happens?"

"Through saliva or blood, we can learn your genetic background."

"You call this marking?"

"It helps us choose a mate."

"How romantic." I can't believe I'm just now hearing this, and he knows who my father is!

"I was going to talk with you about it tonight," he says, and I know he's telling the truth, so I let it slide. I dig around in my bag looking for my phone. It's 11:30. Time for me to go home. I look at my newfound brother. He really looks a lot like me actually. We have the same hazel eyes and thick dark hair. I'm also amazed that his nose shows no sign of injury.

"I hope you don't get into trouble," I say to Yemo.

"Don't worry, Anah. It was worth it."

I feel compelled to hug him, and then I do. It doesn't feel strange. In fact it's only odd how natural it feels.

Slippery Slope

I take off my witch costume and my torn spider-hose and throw on a t-shirt. I give my teeth a quick run around and return to my bed. Victor sits next to me. I remove a piece of werewolf hair from his face. He brushes a strand of my hair to the side. The juxtaposition of experiencing energy from its source at the Halloween dance, and then encountering my twin brother that my boyfriend got into a bloody fight with has tired me. It's a lot to take in.

"You're sad," says Victor.

"Just tired," I reply with a sigh.

"But something else is bothering you."

"I'm surprised, is all."

"Surprised that you have a brother?"

"I'm surprised that advanced beings are still fighting each other. I had a notion that if there were intelligent and spiritually advanced beings there would be peace. I guess that's why I'm sad... because I was wrong."

"I've disappointed you then."

"I guess that's what it is."

Victor lies down on his side and props his head up with his hand. "Unfortunately, there's still a need to fight and conquer. Monahdah's goal is to conquer evil, and we will fight and risk death to preserve what is good and decent. When I pursued Yemo, I did so to protect and preserve good."

"Preserve good?"

"What I mean is you, Anah."

"I don't think I want protection if you're gonna go around beating people up. I don't like seeing people getting hurt, especially you."

"I'm a keeper, and so is Yemo. That is what we do if we must."

"Like Jedi."

"Yes, but we use weapons as a last resort. We confront, negotiate, and if we meet harmful aggression, we can execute. Sometimes the balance becomes unequal."

"What balance?"

"The balance between good and evil."

"Why must there be any evil at all?"

"Maybe someday cruelty for power will be hard to find. Everywhere will be peace and freedom. That's our goal. NeuMonah has found that balance."

"You don't have wars on NeuMonah?"

"Of course not. We don't have poor people like Earth because we don't pay for food and housing."

"So what do you pay for?"

"Nothing. There's no reason to make money."

"How do you get your money to live here?"

"Your government."

"Why does the government give you money?"

"They pay us to stay out of their way and for silence."

This disturbs me. Rather than 'All for one and one for all,' it's survival of the fittest, the one with the most wins and who cares about the rest. Humans are simple. I'm glad now that I'm only half of that *we*.

"*Monahdah try to stay out of the way even though we know we have the power to take over, but that's not our way.*"

"*What about conquering evil? Don't you think we're evil to let people die of hunger and kill each other because they don't have the same religion or belief system?*"

"*Yes and no. Earth is young, and so are its inhabitants. They still have a lot to learn. Adamah... humans are like infants on their evolutionary path as a species. Sometimes the only way to learn is through free will and making mistakes. We're not here to control or to punish. Although some Monahdah actually think we should take over the planet.*"

"*Because we're infants?*"

"*It is our colony for one. It's difficult to watch the power struggles and nuclear threats. Even worse is the complete disregard for the planet, the way people here consume energy just for profit. Knowing there are better, cleaner ways is really hard to tolerate.*"

"*But instead of fighting with other countries you fight with other planets, so, what's the difference?*"

"*True, but we're called keepers because we try to keep peace, not territory, resources or power. Taking over a planet because they*" *aren't doing things for the benefit of all beings is a slippery slope. You've heard this before, 'The road to hell is paved with good intentions.'"*

"So the government knows about you?"

"Us," Victor corrects. *"Yes."* I let that sink in a moment.

"Perhaps you should see how Yemo's doing," I suggest.

"He's fine." He gets that sparkle in his eye as he looks down at me in an endearing way.

"Can you stay until I fall asleep?" I ask.

He lays his head next to mine on the pillow. "Forgive me, Anah, for fighting with your brother. I asked for his forgiveness, but more importantly, I should have asked for yours." His breath is warm on my neck, and I can smell his skin and his sweet breath. His warm hand rests on my side.

"It's okay, Victor. I could never stay mad at you."

The rhythm of his breathing puts me into a slumber. Before I slip into sleep, I catch a glimpse of his thoughts. Soon he will have to leave Earth, and he feels torn about leaving because of me.

Let Him Go

I'm filling out my college application to Stanford. The application deadline is in three days. Mrs. Harvey, the guidance counselor, reminded me today at school. My teachers put pressure on me to apply to Ivy League schools. I wasn't interested in East-Coast schools, so Stanford in sunny California seems like a good choice. I proofread my essay and click send. This time next year I should be a freshman at Stanford.

Despite the changes in my life, I still feel a need to focus on my college education. I was invited to apply last year, but decided to graduate with my class instead. Mom wasn't ready for me to go either. Her stability was disconcerting at the time. I do feel an obligation for her welfare. I hate to admit this, but I will have a harder time than she will. Giving her a reason to wake up in the morning seems like my responsibility. It's what I've always done, and what I'm used to doing.

Where will Victor be while I'm away in college? I already know he won't be here. I look out the window from my desk and stare into the New Mexico night sky. The Milky Way stretches across the sky like a cosmic ribbon. Orion holds his club and shield in the East. If he really cared for me he would stay. If I really cared for him I would be willing to let him go. I feel a lump in my throat. My eyes begin to swell with tears. I didn't think it was possible to feel this way about someone.

Spontaneously, I upload my college application again and click on the University of New Mexico. I upload my essay and click send. I'm surprised, and I'm not sure what my intention is. Going to California no longer seems important. It never was.

Mom comes in the room. "Don't forget your doctor appointment tomorrow."

"Okay," my voice quivers.

Mom turns back to look at me. "Is something wrong?"

As soon as she asks I begin to sob. I wish I could tell her, but I can't. I don't have anyone I can talk to.

"Anah, what is it?" She comes over and puts her arm on my shoulder.

"Everything is happening so fast." I feel uncomfortable opening up to her.

"I understand. It's part of growing up."

"I'm applying to UNM."

"Oh. Well, there's nothing wrong with that. They have a good science program, I hear."

"Victor's leaving, and I'm leaving." I probably shouldn't have said the first part, but it slipped out between sobs.

"Is Victor moving again?"

"Yeah."

Mom hugs me. "I'm really sorry, sweetie."

"What's wrong?" I hear Victor's voice.

"Nothing," I mistakenly say out loud.

"What?" Mom asks.

"I was talking to—I mean, nothing," I say as I sob even more. "Nothing ever seems to go the right way."

"It will. You'll see," she says putting her hand on my back. "I like the idea of you attending school nearby." I smile feeling the same way. It's a relief actually.

"You can come home anytime. You'll only be an hour away, and I can go there to visit too."

"That sounds really nice," I say. She kisses my forehead, and I feel her joy. She's relieved that I was able to open up to her and express my vulnerability. This actually has given her strength. I realize in that moment that I may have been crippling our relationship in an effort to protect her. I guess I'm not as smart as I thought.

Nahmah

I'm reading my book in the bath when I hear Victor send me another mental text. *"On my way over."*

"I'm okay. Victor, you don't need to come over."

"Too late... already here."

I really need to talk to him about this. He doesn't need to come running every time I get a little weepy.

As I dry off, I hear Mom talking to Victor. "I'm sorry to hear that you're moving, Victor."

Oops. I hear silence. *"Just go with it."* I tell him.

"It's not definite."

I take a quick look at myself in the mirror. Wet hair, messy bun. He's seen me look worse.

I make a quick entrance into the kitchen to prevent further inquiries from Mom. "What are you doing here?" I make it sound like a surprise.

"I wanted to see my girlfriend." Victor kisses my damp forehead.

"Are you hungry, Victor?" asks Mom.

"I'm fine, Ms. Weis. Thank you."

"You can call me Beverly, Victor. Ms. Weis makes me sound old. If you get hungry, help yourself to the apple pie I brought home from work."

"Thank you, Ms.—I mean, Beverly."

Victor and I walk back to my room.

"What's this about a doctor's appointment tomorrow?"

"Let's talk normally so my mom doesn't get uncomfortable with too much silence coming from my room."

"Why are you seeing a doctor?"

"To discuss birth control."

"Oh, that won't be necessary."

I'm not sure if I should be hurt by that statement or relieved.

"I will know when it's time to spawn a child."

"There are such things as accidents. Anyway, I should be responsible for my body. This is my body we're talking about here."

"Humans have accidents. Monahdah do not."

"How can *that* be? You don't have sex until you're ready to have a baby?"

"We can have sex, but we control when we release our sperm, and that can only happen once, if we're lucky."

My eyes open wide. "What?"

"We only have one chance to impregnate a mate, so our sperm is extremely valuable to us, as valuable as our mate selection."

"You come to earth to breed, and you mark your potential mates. This is out of necessity. What about love?" I ask, feeling like a science project. "Do Monahdah see love the way humans do?"

He sits next to me, "Love is love. We don't confuse love with needs, yet love is the most confusing things for humans. Sexual expression isn't demonized or considered dirty. It's sensual, spiritual even. A Monahdah's love is everlasting and loyal. We don't have a right or wrong way. We find it strange the way homosexuals are treated here." He kisses my neck then presses his hand against my belly, and we lay back on the bed. He moves his hand up my sweater. Our eyes meet, and I can see the love in his eyes when before it was mostly desire. He presses his body against me and our hands clasp.

"I will return," he says.

"Why are you leaving?"

"To start my training with your father."

That's unfair. I'm losing a boyfriend, and the father I have never known will be with him. Is this what my life will always be like? I feel hurt and betrayed. "When are you leaving?"

"The ship arrives in two moons. We won't leave again for another moon after."

I try to hold back tears.

"I'm not abandoning you, Anah. I know you can be strong and understanding. This is very difficult for me as well."

I think of Mom and wonder if this is what it was like for her. "I should go to my doctor appointment anyway. She wouldn't understand."

"We should respect Beverly's wishes. I'll go with you if that's all right."

I hold his hand. A warm tingling sensation travels up my arm. I study every detail of this moment, because I want it to last forever. The curve of his mouth, the golden tone of his skin. The way his eyes hold light like the ocean at a tropical beach. His cinnamon scent gives me goose bumps. A ripple sensation starts in my heart, and a prickling sensation travels to my brain, letting me know he's about to speak.

He pulls me in close. *"Nahmah,"* he says, and as if I've heard this word all my life, it translates immediately. He's telling me for the first time he loves me. I hold him tightly and say it in return, "Nahmah."

It Only Takes One Time

Why the hell don't they keep it warm in these examination rooms if they're going to make you take off your clothes and wait forever in these paper gowns? I'm waiting for the doctor to make his grand entrance.

There's a quick knock at the door finally, and Dr. Vogel comes in. "You must be Beverly's daughter. It's nice to meet you, Anah." We shake hands, and with my keen sense of smell I detect pot.

"Do you have any questions before your examination?" He opens a manila folder and glances over my file.

"No." Now I smell the coffee he drank to cover up the weed. This is laugh out loud funny. Sophia will love this.

"You would like to be on birth control pills?"

"No." There's a long awkward pause before I realize I should have said yes.

"Are you having sex?" He avoids making eye contact with me.

"My boyfriend and I might be ready for that next step." Every word of that sentence felt and sounded awkward.

"It only takes one time. I'll write a prescription for birth control pills. You have to take one everyday at the same time. You're not protected however for the first month, and you're never protected against sexually transmitted diseases unless he wears a condom." He recites this in an even tone as if it's the fiftieth time he's made that statement today. "It only takes one time," he repeats. He writes on a little white slip. "The nurse will be in shortly to give you an examination."

That's a relief. I wasn't looking forward to a stoned doctor poking me around down there.

The nurse finishes my examination, and it wasn't as bad as I expected. She was really sensitive to the fact that it was my first visit to the gynecologist.

Victor sits in the waiting room reading a Vogue magazine. Women in the room are ogling him. When I enter the room they all pretend they are reading a magazine. *"I guess you're used to woman gawking at you?"*

"Monahdah are handsome. We can't help it."

I laugh as we leave the building.

"I have to stop by the pharmacy to get my pills."

"You don't have to take those you know."

"Mom will know if I don't."

"I had a thought. We should tell her."

"Tell her what exactly?" I wait for him to answer before I open the car door.

"Everything. She already knows about Monahdah, so it's not like she'll think we're crazy."

"What about Yemo?"

"He wishes to meet her. I want to prepare a dinner in her honor."

I'm actually feeling good about this decision. Keeping things from Mom was beginning to wear on me, creating distance between us.

Painful Hidden Memories

Casually we walk through the door. Suddenly I don't know where to begin. Mom is sitting at the kitchen table looking at one of the numerous Christmas shopping catalogues we've recently gotten in the mail.

"Back already," she says surprised. "Everything go okay?"

"Yeah, it was fine." I take my time to unbutton my coat. "Mom, Victor and I want to talk to you about something."

"Don't tell me you're pregnant."

"No, Mom. It's not that."

Victor looks sympathetically at her and says in my head, *"Anah, allow me."*

"Beverly, it has to do with Anah's father."

Mom stares blankly at him, and I can tell she doesn't know what to say. Her eyes shift to mine. I get a strong sense of her emotions before she even does. She feels betrayed and scared.

"His name is MinnEnki, and I know him," says Victor.

Her eyes lock into place. "How do you know him exactly?"

"We are from the same place." Victor allows that to sink in. We sit in silence.

Her breathing becomes heavy and audible. "Is he here?"

"No."

She looks to me and back to Victor, her eyes swelling with tears. "Will he take Anah?"

"No, I don't think so."

"Why are you telling me this?"

"Mom, there's more you should know." I suddenly wonder if this was a good idea. Perhaps it's insensitive to stir up painful, hidden memories.

Victor turns to me. *"Her memory of Yemo has been repressed but I can help her recover them."*

"Mom, I met someone last week." I take a deep breath. "He says he's my brother."

There's a long pause. I sprung it on her too quickly. I'm terrible at this. Mind reading definitely has its advantages.

"I guess your father had more than one woman..."

"My *twin* brother." I nervously curl the corner of a catalogue page. A tear spills over and drips down her cheek. My eyes well with tears because I can feel her pain.

"He said he had to take him," she whispers. "I took turns nursing him and you." Like from a muddled dream, she recovers her memories. "I didn't mind being up all night. I can't remember how old he was when he left... too young to be taken from his mother. Yes... it's coming back to me... I yelled and screamed."

She drifts into her painful memory. I touch her hand and say, "Mommy, it's okay. He wants to meet you. He's here. His name is Yemo."

She looks at me with another memory. "Michael."

"What?"

"I called him Michael."

My Name Is Yemo

Victor has on an apron and dices tomatoes in the kitchen, while Yemo makes several attempts at putting on a necktie in front of the entry hall mirror. Victor dashes to the stove to remove the stir-fry from the heat.

Yemo stares into the mirror and says, "Hello, I'm Yemo, your mother. I mean you're my mother. *I'm* your son. My name is Yemo." Yemo nervously rehearses in the mirror and unsuccessfully ties his necktie on again. "What is the point?"

Victor joins Yemo in the hallway. "I thought you wanted to meet her."

"I mean with these." He whips his tie off his neck.

Victor takes the tie from Yemo and wraps it underneath his collar. "It's how men dress here out of respect." He ties a perfect knot under Yemo's chin. "If I were meeting my mother for the first time I would be just as nervous, but if you're nervous you're going to make everyone else nervous, so just relax."

"They're here." Yemo leaps for the door. Victor put out his arm and stops him. *"I will greet them, after they actually ring the bell."*

The bell rings. Yemo sits down on the sofa facing the fire. Victor opens the door and admires the beauty before him. Anah's cheeks turn red, and he realizes how well her senses have developed. "Beverly, welcome. You look beautiful. It's such an honor to have you as our guest."

"Thank you for giving me a reason to wear a dress."

Victor hugs and kisses me. I smell one of Victor's creations. "Something smells delicious."

Victor looks at me mischievously. *"Not as delicious as you."*

"This is beautiful." Beverly looks around and admires the stone fireplace and sees Yemo.

"Come join us." Victor motions towards Yemo.

Yemo stands. Frozen in a moment of silence, Victor and I wait. I hold my breath. Yemo offers his hand. "Nahmah, Beverly," He says, wearing a big welcoming smile. Beverly takes his hand with both of hers. "I've looked forward to this day for a long time," he says, and the words come out perfectly.

Beverly catches her breath. She wipes away a runaway tear. "You're much taller than I imagined, like your father."

"Hi, Yemo." We embrace.

"Nahmah, Anah."

Mom asks, "What does that mean?"

"That's how Monahdah greet each other. It's similar to how one here would say, 'I love you.' Anah actually means sister." Yemo directs Beverly to sit right next to him. "Technically, though, it means female brother."

"Then how do you say, brother?" asks Beverly.

"Mahna," says Yemo. "You see we are a male species. We don't have women. That's why we revere the women here. When Anah was born after me, Meirlies named her Anah."

"Yemo, slow down. I know you're excited, but you're talking too fast." Anah warns him.

Beverly has a puzzled look on her face. "Meirlies?"

"That means father," says Anah.

"I guess I have a lot of catching up to do."

Victor passes out carbonated drinks in champagne glasses. "To Beverly," he says holding up his glass.

"To mothers," says Yemo.

Everyone clinks glasses.

"Do you know your mother, Victor?" asks Beverly.

"I only know that she lived in Egypt."

"So you never met her?"

"No. She died in a civil war when I was a baby. The fact that you and Yemo are meeting is very celebratory."

"Yes, it is," says a deep voice from behind.

"Beverly, allow me to introduce you to my father, AmanKi."

"Nice to meet you, AmanKi."

"It's an honor." AmanKi reaches for her hand and kisses it. "I see why MinnEnki chose you."

"I use to call him Eric," says Mom.

"You may call *me*, Eamon."

Victor interrupts his father's sudden attraction to Beverly and invites everyone to the dining table. The table setting is beautiful. The center piece is a huge bouquet of lilies and twigs.

He pulls a chair out for me. "My queen."

And Yemo pulls a chair out for Mom. "Beverly."

"It's okay, Yemo. You may call me Mom."

Yemo's big smile turns huge, and his eyes sparkle with delight.

As we eat, I glance around the table and become aware for the first time that I have a family. These are the closest people to me in my life, and it has practically happened overnight. The one thing that would complete this picture is my father. The faint image I have of him gets clearer everyday.

A loud laugh from my mother brings me back to the conversation. I'm unnerved by Mom's flirtatious behavior with Victor's dad. She's blushing and giggling from his flattery. She turns to me and asks, "Do you remember that, Anah?"

"Remember what?"

"Eamon and I were talking about the last time, years ago, when I invited that man, Harold, over for dinner, and you made him really sick. So sick he had to go to the hospital."

"Oh... yes. I don't remember the hospital part, though."

"I guess I better be on my guard then," says AmanKi half jokingly.

Beverly wipes her mouth with her napkin. "How long have you lived here, on Earth?"

"A year," says Eamon.

"And you will stay here indefinitely?"

"We leave when the ship arrives. Other Monahdah will come and stay here."

Mom glances at me and back to Eamon. "And Victor? What about him?"

"He will leave as well."

I don't want to listen to how Victor will be leaving, so I excuse myself to use the restroom. Victor is outside the bathroom door, so I open it. He's standing there with his hands in his pockets with a sad look on his face. "Is everything okay?"

"If it weren't for the constant reminders about you leaving, I would be great."

I look at our reflection in the bathroom mirror and realize that no matter how much I feel complete with Victor, we are separate people, with separate lives.

"Have you noticed my mother flirting throughout dinner with your dad? I'm not used to seeing her behave that way."

"She's at that age," says Victor.

"And?"

"Your mother hasn't had a male companion in a very long time."

"But it's your *dad*."

"Don't worry. He wouldn't do anything unless he cleared it with MinnEnki, out of respect. She's just enjoying the attention. Let her have some fun." He puts his hands around my waist and lifts me up onto the counter. *"Just like you're about to."*

We return to the dining table after we make out in the bathroom. Victor's father stares at my ring. He was too busy flirting with my mother to have noticed it before. *"I noticed,"* he corrects in my head. "This is the ring from MinnEnki?"

"Yes." I extend my hand so he can look closer.

"You were wearing this when you first met Victor."

"That's right," I say.

"It was for her second birthday," adds Mom.

"Wait, you mean, he gave this to you when I was two?"

"Yes, that was the last time I saw him."

"The alloy is actually a plant form. It's a living metal, so to speak," says Eamon. "It looks beautiful on you, Anah." He looks at me again in that mystified way.

"Oh, I didn't imagine it moving when I first put it on." I caress it with my index finger. "Eamon, would you mind showing my mother the pyramid Mon on the mantle?"

"I wouldn't mind."

We all get up to sit around the fire as AmanKi takes the pyramid Mon and hands it to Mom.

"Watch this," says Yemo, and he places his finger on the pyramid. The light travels to his finger and glows and swirls like liquid fire. "It's the same stone as Anah's ring."

"I've never seen anything like it. It's like a captured sun inside. What is it?"

"Condensed astral energy," says Yemo. "You're right. It is like a tiny sun, however this will never die."

"Where did you get it?"

"It's from planet Mon. That's where Monahdah came from originally before we left and colonized other planets like Earth."

"Why did you leave?"

"The planet wasn't able to support us."

"What happened?"

"War. But this was a very long time ago," says Yemo, placing his hand on Mom's shoulder.

"Monahdah don't inhabit the planet anymore?" She says as she gives the pyramid back to AmanKi. She seems to have asked a question that touched a nerve. Yemo, Victor, and AmanKi don't answer the question right away.

"You need not worry, Mom." Yemo smiles at hearing himself call her, Mom.

AmanKi returns the Pyramid back to its place on the mantle. "We no longer control the planet, at least what's left of it. One day Mon will be restored to health and by it's rightful caretakers."

"Can I bring you some tea?" asks Victor, trying to lighten the serious mood.

"We should be going. It's late. But, thank you for a wonderful dinner." Beverly turns to Yemo and places her hands on his arm. She has to look way up to meet his eyes. "Yemo, you can come see me anytime."

"This has been the best day of my life," says Yemo.

"Mine, too." They embrace, and I feel their joy. In that joy I feel parts of me heal, and a wholeness that hasn't been a part of me since I left my mother's womb.

Long Lost Lovers

The drive home, so far, has been quiet. I look over at Mom, and her mind is somewhere else. "Something wrong, Mom?"

"It's nothing."

"I guess it's a lot to digest, all this alien stuff, and seeing your son for the first time, and..."

"I knew my life was going to be different raising you. I didn't know how exactly, but I knew. So none of this comes as a shock."

"Then what is it?" I could pry but decide that she should tell me only if she wants. "I'm lonely," she says wiping away a tear.

"Ah," I say quietly. I wondered when she would admit that not having someone in her life, besides me, wasn't enough.

"Eamon is very charming, isn't he?" I find him intimidating myself, but around Mom he was quite the charmer.

"Yes, I suppose he is."

I don't think I said the right thing. "He's very attracted to you, but how could he not be? You're beautiful, smart, a great person. Anyone can see that."

"While we were alone, he said…" She's too embarrassed to finish her sentence.

"What did he say?"

"That he wanted to tear my clothes off and devour me for dessert."

We both burst into laughter.

"What did you say?"

 "I said, 'Why don't you?'"

"You did? Mom!"

"But he said he couldn't." She turns serious again.

"What did he mean?"

"I don't know. He said something about Eric. Then you, Victor and Yemo came back into the room."

"Victor said something too. They have some kind of strange loyalty to Dad." I park the car in the carport. "I have the impression that he must be a highly respected figure of some kind."

"Well, he has some nerve," she says as she looks out into the darkness.

"Eamon?"

"Your father. I'm mad at him right now. It feels good to take it out on him. It feels good to be angry because it's a feeling other than loneliness."

I turn the car engine off, and the light of the waning full moon shines on my mother giving her face a soft glow. "How did you meet?"

"I was driving home from school and a deer, a young buck, ran right out in front of me. He stood in the middle of the road and stared right into my headlights. I didn't have time to avoid hitting him. It was terrible. He whined and made this terrible sound, in the middle of the road. He tried to get up, but his back legs dragged behind him. I needed to get him out of the road before another car came. Then he appeared, out of nowhere. Your father picked the deer up, carried him to the side of the road, and when he put him down, he got up and ran away."

"The deer was okay?"

"He could barely walk, and then he ran away."

We sat in silence for a moment as I contemplated the fact that this was the first story about my father. He was becoming real and not just a figment of my imagination.

I study the lines on my mothers face that define her and make her even more beautiful. "I'm sorry if this evening upset you."

"I used to feel special, in a weird way," she sighs, "that an intelligent being from another planet chose me. Now I just feel isolated and afraid."

"What are you afraid of?"

"That you'll disappear. That one day I'll wake up, and you'll be gone." She looks out the window at the night sky. "Throughout my day I wonder if he'll just appear out of thin air, like he did the first time. Sometimes I think that I imagined the whole thing. But I couldn't have, right? Because you're real. You, Yemo, Victor... all of this is real." She turns to look at me. "I want things to be different for you. I want you to be happy."

"I am happy."

"Victor will leave soon."

"I can handle it."

"That's the thing, why should you have to?"

"Because I choose to. I have a choice. Just like you do."

We walk into the house. Mom is saying something about my happiness again, but I'm not listening because I suddenly have an overwhelming feeling that someone is in the house. I quickly turn on the light. Standing in the middle of the kitchen is a large man. "You can't stay mad at me forever," he says with a half grin.

Mom drops her purse. She stands there in disbelief. "Eric," she finally says in shock. I am, too. I'm just standing there with my mouth agape.

He's beautiful. He must be close to seven feet tall with dark brown hair, thick and wavy like Yemo's, and hazel eyes like mine. He has on a snug white iridescent pullover and gray pants. His boots are a thin black material forming to his foot like a glove.

"Hello, Beverly."

I'm not sure if Mom is going to slap him or kiss him. He takes a couple of steps closer to her, takes her hand and places it on his face. "Sorry, I'm late."

I look away because I know what will come next. They embrace and kiss like long lost lovers. I clear my throat, and finally their lips part.

"Anah, forgive me for my long absence." He turns to look at me.

"I—I'm…" I'm speechless. He takes my hand with the ring and kisses it. "What do you mean by late, exactly? A month? A couple years?"

"A couple days."

I look at Mom to see her reaction.

"I didn't want you to be disappointed if he didn't show up. I really didn't believe he would."

"You knew he was coming?" I put my hands on my waist.

"Of course not. How was I supposed to really believe that he would show up fifteen years later? I wouldn't want to give you any false hopes."

I do see her point, although I wish she had told me.

"I told you and your mother that I would see you again, if fate allowed, at one hundred and eighty moon cycles."

I look at Mom. Mystery solved. That's what she's keeping track of on her notepad. The numbers coincided with the full moons.

Mom serves tea, and we sit in the living room. Sipping tea he says, "How's Yemo?"

"I hope he's not in trouble," I say.

"For sneaking off without permission? Yes, there will be consequences."

"Is that why you're here? To fetch Yemo?"

"I'm here to see you and your mother. Yemo, I'll deal with him on my own time."

"Why else are you here?" I'm really not trying to sound rude but I can't stop the storm that has been brewing inside me for all these years. A storm that I thought I put behind me.

"To meet with Monahdah and to bring back those who are scheduled to leave." I wonder if this is when Victor is scheduled to leave. "Yes, it is." His voice is firm. "He will."

"Yes, it is, what? Who's he?" asks Mom.

"Victor." He sips his tea. "He'll report back to the ship."

"You mean he has *your* orders to report back to the ship." My sour tone reveals my disappointment.

Mom gives me a sympathetic look. "Anah, like I was trying to say. This is no life for you."

"Mom, I can make my own decisions, thank you."

"Your Mother is right. You have school and a bright future here."

I don't believe it. This man thinks he can just waltz into my life out of nowhere and start telling me what I should do! "And what kind of future is that? One where I'm always looking over my shoulder?" My voice is loud.

He gently places his teacup on the table. "Anah, that's exactly what I don't want for you."

"You didn't have to come all the way from NeuMonah to tell me that!" I stomp to my room and slam the door. I catch my breath. I shouldn't have over reacted. It's too late now. I guess repressed anger has a way of getting out. I feel ashamed and decide to sit on my floor and close my eyes. It doesn't take long to calm the storm inside me. This meditation practice has gotten easier.

When I look up, this strange yet familiar man walks into my room and sits on the edge of my bed. His presence fills in the hazy memory in my mind. His hazel eyes meet with mine. "You're a fast learner."

"Victor taught me."

"I'm sorry for my insensitivity."

"I'm sorry, too." I don't know why, but I kneel down and kiss his hand. "I'm trying to keep up with all the crazy changes in my life."

"You need not ask for my forgiveness." He kneels down and kisses my hand.

Standing on his knees, he's not much shorter than I stand. I wrap my arms around him, and we hug. *"I have a memory of you. You're holding me before you leave, saying that you'll be back."*

"You're even more beautiful than I imagined."

"Thank you." He wipes away my tears. *"Mom is lonely and pretty mad at you."*

"I understand her human needs. Tonight, I will fulfill them."

When he leaves the room, I hear Mom let out a happy laugh that sounds more like a squeal.

I'm not sure if I wanted to hear about Mom's human needs, but I especially don't want to hear what I'm hearing now. I put my headphones on.

MinnEnki's Approval

Maya from Utah waits to speak at the table with fifteen other Monahdah. *"Why are Simerin still within our borders? And why haven't there been any advances?"*

"We'll discuss it when MinnEnki's here and we're all assembled," says AmanKi.

Victor sets out mangos and rice to be polite even though the mood is far from festive. Dressed for the occasion, he's wearing his best clothes from Neumonah. His shirt is white and well fitted. His gray pants are wrapped and tied at the waist. Monahdah don't get nervous, but he feels anxious about seeing Anah's father.

"I would be nervous too, if I were you," says Yemo approaching from behind.

Victor bites into a mango. "I would much rather be me right now than you."

MinnEnki arrives, and AmanKi greets him first. They clasp each other's forearms in a Monahdah greeting.

"Nahmah," says MinnEnki.

"Nahmah, MinnEnki. Good to see you." AmanKi continues in Monahdah. "What can I get for you, dear friend?"

"I think we should start the meeting right away."

"Of course."

Without a spoken word, the men take their seats at the large wooden table.

"You will sit next to me, Yemo," says MinnEnki. "That way I know you won't sneak off somewhere."

"You need to keep an eye on him, not me." Yemo nods to Victor.

He looks directly at Yemo. His hazel eyes pierce into him. *"I have many eyes, Minniedah."*

MinnEnki's words are stern, but his tone is playful. Victor thinks he has Beverly to thank.

"It's a pleasure to see you again, MinnEnki," says Victor.

"I look forward to our private discussion later," MinnEnki says dryly.

Victor swallows a gulp of water from his glass. *"As do I."*

The room is stone quiet, however there's much telepathic chatter. Suddenly, all heads turn and face MinnEnki when he begins.

"Thank you to those of you who were able to arrive on short notice. It wasn't my plan to have an earlier than expected gathering," MinnEnki begins, *"but an issue has become pressing."*

"That must mean a Simerin issue," said RoNh from Arizona.

"I've communicated with them, and they've made it clear that they aren't leaving."

"Why has there not been an attack? It's within our jurisdiction," says RoNh.

"Because they may retaliate with an invasion on this planet if we attack."

"What is their purpose?"

"They want control of Earth," says MinnEnki.

"Why?" asks RoNh.

"Why do we?" asks MinnEnki.

"That's entirely different. We don't actually use force," Fires back MinnEnki.

San from Roswell looks agitated and restless. *"Maybe we should. These humans can't do anything right."*

Maya, representing the Utah clan, turns to San. *"Then perhaps you should return to NeuMonah."*

"I wouldn't look back," spits San.

"They want control of this sector," says MinnEnki. *"If we don't do anything, we still risk an invasion of Earth."*

"Maybe an invasion is what this planet needs," says San.

"How could you think of such a notion?" Victor yells out loud.

San looks at Victor with annoyance and turns to AmanKi. *"AmanKi, please ask your son to control himself. Back to what I was saying, I think it's time we explore negotiating."*

"How do you suggest we negotiate?" MinnEnki asks.

"Let them have Earth or another colony," says San. *"We could ask for Mon in exchange. That would end this immediately."*

"That's exactly what they want, for us to give in to their threats!" Victor catches his breath. "And how would that end anything? There is no end for Simerin!"

"I'm afraid we have no choice. We should plan an attack," says AmanKi, *"before they develop a plan of their own, if it's not too late."*

"I agree. We've been too tolerant," says Maya. *"What terms did you present to them, if any?"*

"I told them they have broken the treaty and if they don't leave they will give us no other choice but to declare war."

"War is apparently what they want," says RoNh.

MinnEnki's eyes suddenly appear ominous with large dilated pupils. The bright green flecks turn several shades darker. *"Then war is what they shall have."*

"We would have to deploy all the keepers from NeuMonah," says Victor.

"They're moving into position as we speak." MinnEnki interlaces his fingers.

"Then so will Yemo and I," says Victor in the midst of telepathic chatter.

MinnEnki stands, and everyone stands in response, saying in unison, "Nos szusahDah ma florah AmanKi." This means, we shall unite and prosper in peace.

The meeting adjourns with heavy hearts. It's been more than sixty Earth years since fighting has taken place between Simerin and Monahdah. The treaty has only provided false hopes of a lasting peace.

MinnEnki approaches Victor. *"It's premature to put you into battle. You still have much training ahead of you."*

"What better way to learn than in battle?"

"I can name several. Mistakes cost lives."

"It's not the way I chose," says Victor, *"It's what was given to me, to all of us."*

"What about my daughter? How would she feel if you were killed in battle because you were ill prepared?"

"She would..."

"She would be devastated, that's what, and she wouldn't have anything to do with me. There's a hotheaded way to go into battle and the proper way. You will first finish your training."

"I am the best flyer."

"With the least experience."

"And what about Anah?" Victor crosses his arms. *"Will she be safe?"*

"Yemo will stay here as her dahman for precautionary measures," says MinnEnki. *"I will discuss that with him."*

Victor senses something strange. Someone has intruded on their conversation. MinnEnki senses it as well. He steps back, peers around the corner of the hall, and San from New Mexico turns away, marching in the other direction.

"Halt! How long have you been listening?" Victor narrows his eyes, waiting for an answer.

"ShanahMi. I was looking for your father."

"He has retired for the afternoon."

"Yes, well then," San bows before he walks away.

"I will prepare breakfast at seven if you care to join us."

"Lamu Nahma." He continues down the hall to his quarters.

Victor turns back to MinnEnki. *"Should we tell the others about Anah?"*

"When the time is right."

"When is that?"

"I will know at the time."

Victor pauses. He wants to ask if he's a proper mate for his daughter.

"I will know that, too, in time."

Girl Time

School is a drag. There's nothing to do now that I'm finished my senior project. I've already got my college acceptance letter from UNM. I got my calculus test back today, and I actually made a real mistake, and it wasn't on purpose.

My life in the past few months has completely changed from boring to outright unbelievable. I have an alien father, an alien twin brother, and an alien boyfriend. Today there's a Monahdah meeting that I can't attend because they don't know about me yet. Shouldn't I be there, too? I have every right to be there. They want to pretend I don't exist, but I do!

Today is also the last day of school before Fall break. I want to spend more time with Sophia. I'm glad she has a boyfriend because I'm starting to feel guilty that we haven't spent much time together. She was pretty upset after the Halloween dance when I disappeared on her. I want to make it up to her and have some real girl time.

Sophia sits down next to me in the cafeteria. "Hey, Soph."

"Hey."

"Are you going to be around during Thanksgiving break?"

"Yeah. You?"

"We never go anywhere. I was thinking that we should get together."

"That would be cool. I'm sure Tim could live without me for a few days."

"What about you?"

"What about me?"

"Could you live without him?" She blows her lips together like a horse. "Of course. I could use a Tim vacation. I feel like his mother."

"So why do you keep seeing him?"

"I guess I like it. It makes me feel important." She takes a swig from her water bottle. "Can I sleep over at your house?"

"That would be great."

Sophia smiles showing her naturally perfect teeth that are the work of God and not an orthodontist.

Chocolate

I'm excited to get home to see my family, however I can't shake an uneasy feeling in my gut. I look forward to hearing about what happened during the Monahdah meeting that my father held.

Victor is by my car door in no time. He opens the door and climbs in to greet me with hugs and kisses. His delicious smell is as intoxicating as always. *"I missed you today."*

"I missed you, too." I'm unable to hear him clearly in my mind, which tells me that he's experiencing tension.

An aroma of fresh-baked cookies greets me at the door. Warm, chocolate chip cookies cool on a baking sheet on the kitchen table. "Thanks for making cookies, Mom," I say looking around at an unfamiliar sight. My house is full of people: Mom, Dad, brother, and boyfriend. I glance at Yemo chewing on a cookie, and he has chocolate on the corners of his mouth, and I laugh.

"What's so funny?" he asks with his mouth full.

"Nothing," I smirk. It's these small moments that I've missed out on for the past seventeen years. He's only fifteen minutes older than me, but I have a feeling I would be the teaser.

"Yemo's never had chocolate before, so I thought I'd make chocolate chip cookies," says Mom cleaning off his face.

Dad sits down, thankfully, because he towers over everyone. Mom looks like a munchkin next to him, and she can't keep her eyes off of him. It's as if she thinks he might disappear at any moment. I see him stare at me from across the room.

"Anah, soon I will have to leave here."

"When?"

"This will be our last evening together before we do."

"You sure have a way of ruining a perfectly good mood," I snap out loud.

"Anah!" yells Mom. "What the hell's that? Maybe you should go to your room."

"Beverly, it's okay," he says. "I need to talk to all of you." We gather in the kitchen around the table. "There's a threat to you, to everyone on Earth."

"What are you talking about, Eric?" Mom says when she sits down.

"It's about the Simerin, isn't it?" I ask sitting next to Victor. "What's happening?"

"Ultimately, they want Earth," says Victor.

"What?" Beverly's frightened voice quivers. "What do they want Earth for?"

"To divide and weaken us," says my father. "They've always felt that Earth belongs to them. They helped colonize Earth millions of years ago. Our genesis scientists were successful, and our descendants evolved and survived, but theirs did not. If they control earth, they don't gain much, but they take away our control and our power."

Yemo bites into a warm, gooey, chocolate chip cookie, seemingly unnerved. Mom pours some milk. Her hands tremble. "Your descendants Survived?" she asks.

"Adamah, the humans that populate Earth today have survived. There wasn't always one human species," Eric continues.

"What does all this mean?" Mom asks horrified.

"We have to stop them," answers Yemo.

"This means you're leaving." She crosses her arms.

"Yes, as soon as possible. We've begun to move into position," says Eric.

"There's going to be war some where up there, over Earth?" Mom's eyes swell with tears. "It's possible we may never see you again."

Father stands up from his chair. "If we don't stop them, war is possible, but we'll do our best to stop it from developing into one."

"All of you are leaving?" I ask.

"Not all," says Yemo.

I take a sip of my milk and stop short. *Will Victor stay?*

"I stay," says Yemo chewing a cookie.

I look at Victor, and he doesn't look at me in the eye.

"Why Yemo?"

Father puts his hand behind Yemo's chair. "You need extra protection. No one knows about you, and we don't trust anyone else right now. I trust Yemo to keep you safe."

"What about Victor? Who will keep him safe?" I raise my voice.

"He's a keeper, Anah. He will finish his training, and he may or may not go into battle."

I feel a knot in my throat but I manage to say, "He could die."

"It's the risk we take. Do you understand?" he asks gently, and my heart receives the message. However, knowing the risk and accepting it are two different things. Victor reaches for my hand, and I hold it tightly. Deep inside, I know he has a bigger purpose, and I'm unsure if I can sense our future together. This is troubling, and I wonder if there's a way I could secure the future that I want.

Abandoned

Victor enters my room. "My departure is sooner than I anticipated."

I'm hurting inside, but I knew this day would come, just not this soon. "I know."

"I'll be back, Anah."

"You don't know that."

He sits next to me. "Please don't think that I won't return."

"What should I do in the meantime while you, my dad, and your dad are off saving the world?" I ask, feeling very alone and abandoned.

"Yemo will be here. You'll go to college and finish your studies."

"That seems pointless now."

"We'll take care of the Simerin. Don't have concern over that."

"What I mean, Victor, is I want to be with you."

He stares into my eyes like he's searching for an answer. He brushes my hair to the side and kisses me. I kiss him back, climb onto his lap and press him back onto the bed.

"You're ovulating," he says in my head while we kiss.

"So let's do it," I say excitedly.

"Are you asking me to mate with you?"

"Yes, right now." I'm so excited I begin to shake. *"Perhaps that's what's supposed to happen."* I press my body to his, and I

want him to want me even more than I want him. He pushes me over and rolls on top of me. *"Are you sure?"*

"I've never been so sure about anything."

Victor sits up and moves away. "What's wrong?" I ask.

"Your father—," he begins to say.

"This is none of his business."

"I may not be a suitable mate for you."

"That's ridiculous. You are, and I don't care what he says. Perhaps you don't find me suitable."

"You're more than suitable. Anah, I don't think you understand."

"I understand that you're leaving, and I may never see you again. Now you're rejecting me."

"This is in no way a rejection. This is waiting." He holds my face and says out loud, "I want to be there when our child is born. If we do this now, I wouldn't be."

I realize I'm behaving selfishly and overreacting to his departure.

"Anah, will you wait for me?"

Our foreheads touch, and we close our eyes. I feel our spirits embrace.

"I'll wait."

"Nahmah," he says.

"Nahmah."

In The Darkness

When people can read your mind, and you can read others', you need to find solace. The creek sparkles with half moonlight, and I feel comfort in the darkness that surrounds me. There's a change going on inside me, emotionally, biologically, and spiritually. It all seems to be connected, and there's a force guiding me. Perhaps it's the force of my own path that I didn't notice before.

I'm glad Victor had the strength to make the right decision. I was emotionally vulnerable. He could have taken advantage of that. With a clear mind I realize it's not time. I look up into the night sky at the innocence of the glimmering stars. I don't want to think of the world differently than how it is in this very moment; safe, and secure from the harmful will of an alien race unbeknownst to its inhabitants. If Victor must leave to secure this peace… and I may never see him again, then I must accept that outcome, that sacrifice. A new sensation of strength grows in the pit of my belly. This gives me courage to let him go. Now, more than ever, he needs my support. A large meteor shoots across the sky with a long tail of bright purple and green then orange, memorializing this moment.

Like A Woman

I'm waiting in Victor's room. At the request of our fathers, we agreed that it still isn't time to introduce me to the Monahdah community. I guess that means they don't entirely trust everyone. There's about a hundred Monahdah here wandering around the property. Most of them will leave with the ship to help in the battle against the Simerin or make their way back home to NeuMonah. I won't be able to see him off because it would draw too much attention, so this is where we we'll have our last goodbye.

"Anah?" I hear Victor call.

I'm in his shower smelling his shampoo and soaps in search of that cinnamon scent he wears. "I'm in here."

"It might help to turn the water on, and take your clothes off."

"I was just, well, I was..."

"Is this what you're looking for?" He presses against me and wraps his arms around my waist. I bury my face into his chest, and the delicious scent invades my nose.

"Yeah, what is that?"

"It's just the way I smell to you. You're not going to find it in a bottle."

I look up at him and know this may be the last time I see him. I wish I had words that could sum up everything I feel. I want him to know about my new sense of courage and faith that we'll be together again.

"It's okay, Anah. You don't need to say anything. I hear your feelings." He places my hand on his heart. When we embrace I experience something new. I'm no longer a girl because I feel so much like a woman.

"I want to give you something," he says as he walks to the shelf above his bed.

"I have something for you, too. But you can go first."

"Put out you hand and close your eyes," he says.

I put out my hand, and he places something there. "Okay. Open your eyes." I open my eyes and see Victor's Oldsmobile keys. "Are you actually giving me your car?"

"It's yours."

I'm smiling ear to ear. "This is an awesome gift, Victor!"

"Look at the key chain," he says, pointing. The key chain says, 'I like to go fast.' "Thank you. I promise to take good care of it."

"What's your gift?"

"Well… it's not as good as a car." I reach into my pocket and pull out a necklace that I made from the leather and the turquoise bead I bought at the village of Cerrillos. He ties the leather cord at the back of his neck. The turquoise bead hangs just below the indent of his neck by his collarbone. We stand in silence, and I admire one last time his facial features, his defined jawline, his aqua eyes framed with his thick caramel colored brows, and the dip in his chin that leads to his lips. Our foreheads touch. When I open my eyes, he's gone.

Blessings

It's Thanksgiving, and the house smells like turkey and sweet mashed potatoes. Despite the fact that my recently discovered father and my boyfriend are preparing to go to war with Simerin, I have a lot to be grateful for. I'm especially happy that Sophia is here to celebrate with me, Mom, and Yemo. She's staying overnight, and I'm looking forward to quality girl time.

She thinks Yemo is my cousin. Lying makes me extremely uncomfortable, especially since I know when someone isn't telling the truth, but it will avoid questions that I'm not ready to answer. How would my best friend react if she learned that I wasn't human but a hybrid created by an alien race? She would never look at me in the same way. One day she will know, but that's not today.

We're setting the table in the dining room. The last time I set the table in here was at Christmas. While folding the napkins, I notice that Yemo keeps staring at Sophia.

"Have you a mate, Sophia?" Yemo leans against the wall and crosses his arms.

"Yemo!" I snap.

"A mate?" Sophia sets a fork and knife down on a napkin. "What does he mean?"

"Yemo, the word is boyfriend. It's a little weird, just so you know, to say mate."

"Your cousin is a little weird," Sophia whispers in my ear.

"Why don't you go see if Mom needs help in the kitchen?"

Yemo leaves the room a little embarrassed, and I feel bad for yelling at him.

"Yemo, try running something by me first before you open your mouth. That way you'll avoid embarrassment."

"Monahdah don't get embarrassed."

"Whatever. I'm just trying to help."

"Stubborn," I mumble.

"What?"asks Sophia.

"Nothing. Sorry about Yemo. I'll ask him to stop bothering you."

"That's okay. He's weird, but why didn't you tell me you had a super hot cousin?"

"I, ah, well, never looked at him that way before. You know, he's my cousin."

Mom brings in the turkey, and Yemo carries the potatoes in one hand and pineapple casserole in the other. Sophia and I help put out the cranberries and creamed onions, and then we take our seats. Mom wants us to hold hands so she can say a blessing. Yemo reaches for Sophia's hand. She gladly accepts without hesitation.

Mom begins. "I'm thankful for the safety of our families and friends and for the food that we are about to eat." Sophia says that she's thankful for the opportunity to share Thanksgiving with me and the family. Yemo says he's grateful for being with his new family. I clear my throat not knowing what to say.

"I'm grateful that we live in a time and place where families can come together in peace and in health, where we can share our ideas and our dreams with the free will to pursue those dreams without oppression, without fear and with the hope that when everyone else has that we can all live closer to our perfect selves." The room becomes quiet and the ticking sound of the clock sounds louder than usual. Mom wipes away a tear.

"Oh, and Anah, thank you for bringing my future PrimonKi to Thanksgiving."

"Yemo, you don't know if she's your future mate or not, so just cool it. Pass the potatoes, please!"

"When does Victor get back from his trip?" Sophia says breaking the silence.

"His father has a lot of business to do in Europe and Asia, so they'll be gone awhile."

"Like what kind of business?"

"He's an antiques dealer, mostly cars."

"Victor has the coolest car." She blows on the hot potatoes. "That's so cool he let you have it while he's gone. What kind of car is it?"

"It's an Oldsmobile." It puts a lump in my throat thinking of Victor, so I want to change the subject. Yemo knowingly cuts in.

"Sophia, if you prefer to sleep in my room that's fine with me," he says.

"Yemo..." I warn.

"Where would *you* sleep?" Sophia asks.

"In my room, of course."

I try to laugh it off like it's a joke, but I know he's perfectly serious.

"Yemo, sweetie, the girls will sleep in one room, and you will sleep in another." Mom chimes in.

"Tell her you're joking, please," I say.

"Joking?" he asks unsure of the meaning.

"That you're not serious, that you didn't really mean it!" I telepathically yell.

"Of course I mean it. I don't want to insult her."

"Eat your turkey." I roll my eyes.

"No, thank you. We don't digest other beings," he reminds me.

"Well, there's plenty of other things to eat," says Mom.

Sophia says while cutting her meat, "What do you mean, 'we?' He said, 'we.'"

"His family is vegetarian," I say and give Yemo a warning glance.

"Are you religious or something?" asks Sophia.

"Yeah, they're Buddhist," I say. "Right, Mom?"

"This month," Mom says as she surprisingly plays along.

I try to think of something that we could talk about that won't involve lying. "Did you decide on what college you want to go to, Sophia?"

"I'm thinking about taking some time off from school."

"What would you do instead?" Mom asks.

"I want to travel."

"By yourself? That's not very safe, Sophia."

"Anah could do it with me."

"Sounds tempting." I mix my corn into my mashed potatoes. "I can't wait 'til graduation."

"Yeah, me too! I'm totally done with high school." Sophia takes another bite and blushes when she notices that Yemo has been intently staring at her. "Are you going to college, Yemo?"

"I will go where Anah goes." Sophia looks at me sidelong with an expression that says, 'what the hell?'

"You can go wherever you want, Yemo. He's just being weird on purpose," I say to cover up my embarrassment. "Mom, everything's delicious. I think I need a break before dessert." I want to hang out with Sophia privately in my room.

"Alright. That'll give me time to warm up the apple pie."

We put our dirty dishes in the sink, and I lead Sophia to my room. "Sorry about my cousin," I say as I shut my door.

Sophia checks herself out in my bedroom mirror, which is leaning against the wall. "How long will he be visiting?"

"He might move in with us, actually. His home life isn't very stable, and we offered for him to stay here for a while."

"I guess it would be nice for you to have a guy around. You know, to help out around the house when things break." She plops down on my bed holding her full stomach. "He looks freakishly strong. He must work out a lot." Sophia drifts off into lustful thoughts.

"Sophia, stop. You're drooling."

"Sorry, Anah, but I'm totally hot on your cousin, and he smells so delicious, I want to eat him."

"Really? What does he smell like?" I ask, wondering if he smells anything like Victor.

"I don't know... it's like a mixture of orange spice and chocolate."

"Oh." I wonder if this is some Monahdah trick to attract women. "Are you tired of Tim?"

"Just bored, I guess," she says, twirling a lock of her hair. "We'll break up soon, anyway. I don't want to have a steady boyfriend after high school. I want to be free as a bird."

"Does he know that?"

"No. I'm not ready to talk about it yet with him. I do care about his feelings."

I sense Yemo's presence outside my bedroom door, and then he knocks. "Come on in, Yemo."

"I want to ask Sophia if she would like to sit with me as we watch a movie."

Sophia's cheeks flush.

"I don't know if Sophi—"

"What movie do you want to watch?" Sophia says, excitingly. So much for girls' night.

"I'm not sure if I care what we watch," he says.

"Thanks, Yemo. We'll be there in a minute. Why don't you cut Sophia a piece of that pie?"

"Excellent idea, Anah."

Mission Impossible

We squeeze together on the couch with Sophia in the middle and watch Mission Impossible. Yemo mostly watches Sophia and keeps feeding her pieces of pie.

"She's not a toy. Stop feeding her."

"I'm showing her signs of my affection. Didn't Victor do this with you?" I was about to say, of course not, but then I remember tasting the honey from Victor's finger. *"Not on the first date."*

"But he did, didn't he?" He spoon-feeds her another bite.

I drift off and remember sitting in Victor's car when he let me taste the honey from his finger and just then, I sense him. He's thinking of me. I close my eyes and take a deep breath. I can smell him as if he's sitting right next to me. My heart starts to beat faster.

"What's so impossible about that?" Yemo comments on what's happening in the movie. "That's mission easy."

"You're not impressed?" asks Sophia.

"Of course not, I could do that with my eyes closed."

"Yemo, to most people here, these are remarkable feats."

"He's joking again," I say to Sophia.

"Joking? Oh, right... joking," he says dipping his finger into the apple pie.

Sophia looks at Yemo quizzically. "Are you really joking?"

Yemo moves his finger to Sophia's lips, and she licks the pie from his finger. "Perhaps," he says.

"Thanks for the idea, Anah." I roll my eyes. I return my thoughts back to Victor to see if he's still there, but he's gone. I wonder again if I'm strong enough to handle this, and I tell myself I am.

Yemo suddenly stands. "Let's go outside. I want to look at the sky and see what it looks like here."

"Wouldn't it look the same here as it does anywhere?" asks Sophia.

"It's pretty cold out," I protest.

"I'll keep my girls warm. Don't worry."

He grabs a blanket from his room, and we climb onto the roof from his bedroom window.

We snuggle under the blanket and look up at the dark moonless night.

"See that red star?" Yemo asks me. *"The red one there?"* His eyes show me the direction in the sky.

"Aldebaran?" I ask. *"What about it?"*

"That's home... NeuMonah. You can't see the planet, but that's our star."

"How do you travel between here and there?"

"Your scientists call them wormholes. One exists between this solar system and NeuMonah."

"So it makes intergalactic travel between here and there possible?"

"It takes light 65 years to travel the 382 trillion miles. With your current technology it would take your scientist close to 40,000 years to get there."

"How long is a NeuMonah year?"

"One year for NeuMonah is about nineteen Earth moons."

"You two are quiet," says Sophia.

"Are you warm, Sophia?" asks Yemo.

"I'm a little cold," she says wanting attention.

"The sky is very pretty here, but lonely at the same time," says Yemo.

"Lonely?" asks Sophia. "What do you mean?"

"Earth is far from anything. It's like being in the middle of nowhere."

"Would you travel in space if you could?" Sophia asks.

Yemo laughs. "That's like me asking you if you would get in your car and go to town."

"Yemo," I warn him again.

"What I mean is, yes, of course I would," he corrects. "Would you?"

"No, I don't have any desire to venture out into the dark unknown."

"Space exploration isn't for everyone," he says.

"What about you, Anah?" Sophia asks.

"Sure, why not? I'd like to go and see other worlds."

"Even if it meant you may never come back?"

I was about to say, If it meant I could be with Victor again.

Yemo puts his arm around me. *"You will, Anah. One day, you will."*

I try to search for Victor in my future, but that picture is still very dim. Maybe it's too far away for it to be clear.

Knock First

I barge into Yemo's dorm room in a panic. He's making out with some girl with her shirt off, and he has his hands on her bra strap trying to unhook the clasp.

"What the hell!" she screams. "You said you didn't have a girlfriend!"

"That's my sister."

"Cousin," I correct.

"I mean, cousin."

The girl puts her shirt on. "Nice try," she says as she scurries out of the room.

I shut the door behind her. "Something's wrong!"

"Damn skippy!" Yemo snaps using his newly learned lingo. "I was occupied, if you didn't notice!"

"Yeah, what else is new?"

"You could at least knock first, Anah."

"Ok, next time try locking the door." I plop down on his bed.

Yemo starts to speak to me telepathically. *"What's wrong?"*

"He's not answering."

"Since when?"

"Last night sometime."

"Can you sense him at all?"

"I sense nothing."

"Give it more time. Try not to panic. You should have some kind of code between you."

"What do you mean?"

"If he communicated to you while taken prisoner, he would jeopardize your life and possibly the future of the universe."

"Must you always remind me?"

"You need a code, you see." He puts on his t-shirt.

Yemo and I are in our first semester at the University of New Mexico. He enjoys college life and has no problem with the girls and finding cool parties, as to be expected from Monahdah.

Victor finished his training on one of the space stations not far outside the Earth's atmosphere and was sent recently on his first mission in the conflict with the Simerin.

I sit on the edge of his bed. "Like what?"

"Like anything." Yemo leans back on his desk chair. "He could answer by saying, the temperature is very hot in here, to mean, I can't talk right now, knee deep in shit, etc."

The sky darkens outside his dorm room window as a single cloud passes in front of the sun. "Yemo, what will happen if we lose?"

"We will leave."

"To where?"

"NeuMonah, of course."

"What about everyone else, the rest of the planet?"

"We would take as many as we can with us."

I pause. *"How many would that be?"*

"We can fit fifty-thousand on one ship and another ninety-thousand on the big ship."

"That's only a hundred and forty-thousand! What about everyone else?"

"They would perish. We have another ship currently on its way, but it will take ten Earth years before it will arrive. Its mission is to rescue any survivors, should we lose."

"In ten years?"

"Humans are adaptable. They could survive that long if they are ready."

"As slaves to an alien race."

"They could go into hiding. Most would be killed or just die from starvation."

I'm pacing from one side of the room to the other which is only five feet of space. "You say that so easily, like it's a normal every day event for billions... an entire planet, to get wiped out."

"It's not that I don't care about humans, despite their lack of awareness. I would as a Keeper, sacrifice my body for one."

"Because that's what you're trained to do," I say with bitterness in my voice.

"Yes, but also because we maintain order in the universe, not just for beings of Earth, but for all beings everywhere in the universe."

I realize I'm choosing to argue because of my own frustration, and I'm going to be late for class. I put on my backpack. "Talk to you later, Yemo."

"We're going home this weekend," he says as I'm walking down the other end of the hallway on my way out the door.

"Are you asking or telling?"

"Telling. Sophia will be home."

That's terrific. He knows the status of my best friend before I do. I would warn Sophia to stay away from my brother, since he's a player with the girls, but she already knows. In fact, he tells her everything, and she does the same.

"I'll talk to you about it after class." I pick up my pace so I won't be late.

I've had guys ask me out, but it's weird. I really don't have any interest in them. Yemo is so protective of me that most guys are afraid to ask me out. Alan, from my physics class, was going to ask if I would meet him for coffee. Yemo showed up out of nowhere and managed to scare him off without even trying. I felt really bad. Alan's a shy, cute physics geek, and it took him several days to get up the nerve to talk to me. Maybe I'll talk to him after class today. I haven't really made any friends here, and I'm beginning to feel alienated.

My thoughts return to Victor, the way they usually do. His absence is tolerable, since I've learned to telepathically communicate with him. Sometimes it's just his scent, his touch, or a kiss. At first, I thought I was hallucinating or that my mind was playing tricks on me, but, well, the night before last was no hallucination. I walk into class with a dreamy grin on my face thinking about it.

You Left Your Position

Victor pursues a Simerin fighter craft when three more Simerin fighters appear out of nowhere. He's outnumbered and dangerously out maneuvered. His fighter is taking a lot of hits, but his shields haven't been penetrated. He maneuvers his fighter straight up and reverses. Victor has excellent combat instincts. He can read his opponent's moves and create traps that give him the upper hand. Now he's behind all three fighter crafts. His fire rains down on them hellishly. The Simerin ships explode one by one, and Victor smiles out of the corner of his mouth since he out smarted and out maneuvered them. An alarm goes off. His fighter is damaged, and he must return to the station before it's too late. He looks at his location and realizes how far off he is. He ignored orders to stay within his assigned district since he didn't want to lose his target.

He asks for permission to return and gives his entry identification code.

As he exits his fighter on the landing dock, another Keeper approaches him. "Report to MinnEnki."

"After I..."

"Now."

He knew there would be repercussions and prepares to hear them as he enters the commander's room.

"You left your position, Victor. I have fighters in district two and in district three. You went as far as district four and only luck returned you," says MinnEnki.

"Then how did that ship get to my district?"

"It could have been a decoy. You left your position and the ship vulnerable."

"I took down four Simerin fighters," Victor says wanting recognition despite his negligence.

"When your fighter is repaired you may go back. Remember, eagerness reveals a beginner."

"This whole thing could be a decoy," says Victor before walking away. "All our focus is here, and in the meantime they could be heading for Earth."

"Keepers are scouting. Focus on the assignment given to you," says MinnEnki. "Meanwhile, you must wait for your fighter to be repaired."

"That could be awhile."

"Yes, it could."

The Coffee Shop

I push my way through a crowd of college students, shuffling around the hallway on our break between classes.

"Hey, Alan."

"Hi, Anah." He avoids making eye contact.

"I was about to head over to the coffee shop. Do you want to go?"

"Wouldn't that piss off your giant boyfriend?"

"He's my cousin."

"Oh... then, wouldn't that piss off your giant cousin?"

"Of course not. He'll probably be there, though. Don't worry, he's harmless."

"Well… okay."

"We can head over right now, if you want."

He swings his backpack on. "Okay."

The coffee shop is packed with college students. Alan and I get in a long line to order. Yemo's at a table chatting away with another couple. He always finds someone to talk to, and everyone seems to know him.

Alan and I finally order, and I point out which table to grab. He wears a doubtful look on his face. A couple sits there quietly typing away on their laptops. "That table isn't available as you can see."

"They're leaving," I say confidently,

He looks over again, and they close their laptops and put their coats on.

"See," I say with a grin.

"How'd you do that?"

"Do what?" I ask as I set the coffee mugs on the table.

"You knew those people were leaving."

I take my cell phone out of my back pocket before I sit down, and I place it on the table. "Lucky guess."

"Here comes your cousin," Alan says nervously.

"Yemo, this is Alan." I blow on my hot coffee before taking a sip. "What are you up to over there?"

"We were discussing football," says Yemo sitting down.

Alan nervously taps his coffee cup. "Are you a football player?"

"No, it's an archaic sport." Yemo takes off his wool scarf. "Just like these trendy scarves. It doesn't interest me."

"Then why are you wearing it?" I ask.

"It was a gift from Sophia."

Alan quickly scans Yemo's physique. "You look like you play football or something like it."

"Maybe I'll join this ice hockey team. It's interesting the way they maneuver on those shoes."

Sending a telepathic whisper, I say, *"They're called skates, Yemo."*

I look over at Alan, and he doesn't know what to think of him. "See, I told you he's harmless."

Without warning, I sense alarm coming from Yemo. He's intensely scanning the room. It's filled with different groups of college students on laptops and cellphones, but then he notices an out-of-place character.

Alan raises his eyebrow. "What's with him? He suddenly looks like the Terminator."

"What's wrong, Yemo?"

"Communicate like a human," Yemo says in a low stern voice, "or not at all."

"Sorry," says Alan. "The last time I checked, I was human. Although, I do find myself wondering at times if I'm more advanced—"

"You're not. Now quiet. I wasn't talking to you."

Alan looks at me a little confused. "I'm not human? Or not advanced?"

Yemo grabs his scarf and leaves the table. "Stay here, Anah."

"Does he always talk like that?" Alan asks.

A man quickly leaves the coffee shop, and Yemo follows after him.

"Your cousin is strange, to say the least," says Alan before drinking his coffee.

"I'll be right back." I hastily leave the coffee shop and catch a glimpse of Yemo crossing a street at a busy intersection. The traffic light turns green then immediately turns back to red, and cars come to a screeching halt. I run across the street just before the light turns green again. I wish I knew how to make myself invisible at will. It's something that only happened that one time when I caught my teachers having an affair. This would be an ideal time for it to happen again. I don't want to piss off my brother for following him, but more importantly, I could put myself and Yemo in jeopardy.

He turns down an alley, so I slow down my pace as I approach the corner. I peak around the corner into the alley. Yemo leaps and tries to grab the stranger. The man disappears right before my eyes, and a rat scurries down a drain. "Did he just turn himself into a rat?" I ask making my presence known.

Yemo turns around with an alarming expression. "We need to leave," he says, grabbing my arm.

"Do you know him?"

"Not really, but now he knows you, and that's why we must leave."

"He's Monahdah. Why would he be running away?"

"He's a drohan."

"He's not Monahdah?"

"I don't know the translation for drohan. It's when you think someone is good, but they aren't, and they can't be trusted."

"Oh, then he's a traitor or a double crosser. You've seen him before?"

"Yes, at the house of AmanKi. He's San from the New Mexico band in Roswell."

"What's the big deal if he knows about me, anyway? I don't see what harm it could do me. Why would another Monahdah have bad intentions?"

"I don't know. He did well to protect his deception."

I raise my eyebrow. "Deception?"

"What?"

"You know the word deception but not traitor?"

"I just learned that word today while discussing football. Long story...not important." He pulls me along by my arm at a fast pace, crossing the road. "Thanks for helping me out back there with the traffic light. Although, you should have stayed put like I instructed."

"Where the hell are you taking me?"

"To my pod."

"Your what?"

"The ship."

I'm pretty sure I heard correctly, but I ask again. "Come again?"

"I'm taking you home."

"We can use my car for that. It's only an hour and a half away."

"Not to Mom's house. I'm taking you to NeuMonah."

"Woah!" I halt, pulling my arm away from his grip. "I'm not leaving the planet. Are you nuts?"

Yemo grabs both of my arms and looks at me square in the face. "Anah, when are you going to accept the fact that you are not one of these people? You're Monahdah."

"Can't I just transfer schools? This seems like a drastic decision."

"They'll keep finding you. Neumonah is the safest place now."

"What about Mom?" I ask, feeling like I'm about to cry.

"If we go there, it might put her in danger. They can get from her any information we tell her. The less she knows the better."

That's when it hits me, really hard, for the first time, or maybe second. My life will never be the same.

"I need to go to my dorm to get my things."

He pulls me along. "There's not enough time."

"Yemo, the worst thing to do is panic. If you want to take me to NeuMonah that's fine, but I'm not leaving without my things."

"Fine. Get what you want... make it snappy."

I open the door to my dorm room, and it's completely ransacked.

"He was here," says Yemo.

"My ring!" I pray it's not missing. The box I keep it in is open on the bed and it's gone.

"Meirlies gave me that ring." I throw the empty box on the bed.

"We'll get you another one. Now let's go." He nervously looks out my dorm room window. "Is there anything else you want?"

"My favorite jeans, Victor's t-shirt... What do I need exactly? How long will it take to get there?"

"In Earth time, or NeuMonah time?"

"I don't really care. Earth time, I guess."

"One earth year."

"What?" At least he didn't say six years, or sixty-five.

"Maybe more. We have to meet a ship, and then it depends."

My insides quiver. "On what?"

"On the ship. Let's go! We'll have plenty of time to talk later."

"Yeah, twelve months or more." I squeeze my jeans into my backpack. "I can't leave the room in this condition. People will think I was killed."

"It's a dorm room. They won't know the difference."

I stuff a few more items into my backpack: my hairbrush, toothbrush, a box of tampons. I realize that I'm shaking and holding back tears. Yemo takes ahold of my hands, places them on his heart, and looks straight into my eyes. He speaks to me in Monahdah. *It will be okay. Will you trust me?* Yemo has a very special gift. I instantly feel the strength from his heart. Even though I don't speak Monahdah yet, I understand.

"Yes," I say. He wraps his arms around me, and my fear washes away.

We Make a Good Team

Victor's Oldsmobile is parked near my dorm. I unlock my car door, throw my backpack onto the backseat, and reach over to manually unlock the passenger door for Yemo. "You know how to get to your pod?"

"Just start driving north. I'll tell you where to go. It's not far from Mom's house."

"We can leave the car at the house then."

"We can't leave any traces that would lead them to Mom."

"Victor gave me this car to take care of. He's trusting me with it."

I get on the highway and drive in the direction of Santa Fe.

"We'll figure something out. Have you heard from Victor?"

"No. Not at all."

"He's fighting in a war to save the planet, last I heard," says Yemo rolling down the window a little.

"I know what's going on, and I'm not upset about it anymore. I'm fine."

Yemo keeps turning around to look behind us. I look in the rear view mirror to see what he's looking at. "What is it?"

"There's a car following closely behind us."

I speed up and pass the car in front of us. The white sedan behind us does the same.

"Shit. He's following us?"

"Yes. You need to lose him. How fast can this go?

"Fast," I say and press harder on the gas peddle. I speed by car after car, easily going 90. I look back, but he's still right behind us.

"Can't you go any faster?" Yemo yells. "He's right on our ass!"

I press the pedal to the floor. We're going over 100 now.

Yemo rolls the window up and says, "We're going to have to jump!"

My eyes open with fright. "Out of the car?"

"Take my hand!"

When I take his hand I understand what he wants to do. I did the same thing during my race with Victor. We both focus on being in front of the cars that are ahead of us. If it doesn't work we'll cause a huge accident, slamming into the car in front of us. For two seconds, it feels like we're submerged under water. When I hear a loud pop, I open my eyes. The cars that were in front of us are now almost a mile behind.

Yemo yells out like a cowboy and says, "That was an awesome jump, Anah!"

I break to make a quick turn. "I know a shortcut."

The county road stirs up a lot of dust as I look through the rearview mirror. "I think we lost him."

Yemo looks at me with fondness. "We make a good team. That was the biggest jump I've ever done."

"Really?"

"You have to be careful though. You can jump too far and have trouble getting back."

"From where?"

"Another dimension, time, place. You could jump to a whole other time line."

"How do you get back?"

"You can try to get back the same way if you remember what happened. I've never jumped that far. Sometimes there's a glitch, and you don't realize you jumped. I'm sure you've experienced it before in a brief moment. You experience a time skip, and you say that French phrase."

"Déjà vu?"

"Yeah, that one." Yemo looks around. "We need to get rid of the car."

"Wait! This is Victor's car, and I promised to take care of it."

"We'll find a place to hide it. We don't have a choice. I want to go the rest of the way on foot."

We turn down another dirt road and hide the car behind some piñon trees. I feel terrible about leaving the car here. I swing my backpack over my shoulders, hide the keys under the hood and hike out into the piñon forest.

Feeling Helpless

Like a heartbeat drives you mad
In the stillness of remembering what you had and what
you lost and what you had and what you lost.
—Fleetwood Mac

"I asked you not to communicate with Anah, for her own safety," says MinnEnki.

Victor places his fist on the table. "I haven't, but I sense something terribly wrong."

"Let's not overreact. She's with Yemo."

Victor leans on the table with both arms. "I want permission to return to Earth."

"Denied. You'll have to trust that she's safe with Yemo and stay focused on our mission here. Your fighter is soon ready. I want you to return to your assignment."

Victor returns to his quarters and changes into his uniform. He sits back on his bed and stares up at the ceiling. Perhaps he made a mistake leaving Anah. If something happened to her he wouldn't want to live with himself. Frustration is something he's not familiar with, and he's having a difficult time sorting things out. He dislikes feeling helpless and out of control. He's had too much time on his hands waiting for his fighter, and perhaps getting back will help him to refocus. He squeezes his head with his hands. *"I just need to know if you're safe,"* he says to himself, hoping he will channel her enough to know. *"There's only one way to find out."*

To the Pod

We've been on foot for about thirty minutes. I can smell the fallen leaves drying in the New Mexico sun, and I feel sweat drip down my chest. We've come to the place where Victor let his horse graze that snowy morning on our horseback ride. The day we had our first kiss. It's a good memory, but it makes my heart ache.

I unzip my coat and stop to rest. "How much farther?"

"We're close."

A cool breeze blows, and a cloud passes in front of the sun, offering a welcoming reprieve from the hot sun. Yellow leaves from the surrounding cottonwoods sprinkle down around us. It's been a little over a year since I met Victor and learned that my paternal family comes from another planet. It's amazing how much has changed since then. I miss him. Right now, at this very moment, I want nothing more than to look into his eyes, smell his sweet cinnamon scent, and feel the way he makes me feel— happy, safe, and complete.

"Anah." I hear Victor's voice. I stand and turn aroun

"Victor?"

"I'm here." I march in the direction of his voice. "Victor!"

"Anah! Wait!" Yemo grabs my arm, but I jerk it away.

"It's Victor. He's here!" I run ahead excited that he's come for me. He's always been there for me when he sensed something was wrong, so of course he would now. A strong force from behind knocks me down. I have a mouth full of dry leaves and dirt. I try to break free, but I'm being held down. I can't see my assailants with my face pressed into the ground! I'm now being dragged by my feet.

I kick and scream for help. "Yemo!" There are two of them and characteristically inhuman. They have small mouths, perfectly rounds eyes that recede into their skulls and protruding foreheads. Their skin has a brown-yellow tint, or maybe it's the color of the leaves because they seem to blend into the environment. I'm having my first encounter with Simerin!

Yemo runs straight for us like a mad bull from hell but comes to a screeching halt. One of the Simerin threatens to kill me on the spot if he takes one step closer. Their language sounds similar to Monahdah but not as elegant and more sinister.

"Kill her," instructs the Simerin standing next to the one pinning me down. He digs his elbow into my chest, and I scream out in pain. He puts his face close to mine and sticks out his long, black, fleshy tongue. He smells horrendous! His face is so close, I can feel his warm, smelly breath, and his skin has a smooth, tacky feel.

I remember my dream. All this is similar to what happened in my dream. If I don't do something, like right now, it will be too late. I just need to break free from his hold. It can't be done with force, since I can't move, so I must use my wits. First, I need to calm down, so I can be convincing. Maybe my tricks will save my life.

"I think your friend here likes me. I think I like him, too. If you kill me, we can't have any fun, now, can we?"

I feel him let off some pressure but not enough for me to break free.

"You can take me with you. I'll do whatever you want."

He drags me to my feet and instructs his partner to kill Yemo. He aims his weapon and fires. Yemo takes cover behind a large, cottonwood tree. Wood and bark explode everywhere, and I have to cover my face. The air is filled with smoke and the smell of burning wood.

It's now or never! I slam my boot as hard as I can into my assailant's groin. When he falls forward from the impact, I slam my elbow into his back. I turn to run, but he grabs ahold of my leg and pulls me down. He reaches down with his spindly hands to grab me, and I kick him as hard as I can in the face. I surprise myself to see him fly backward landing flat on his back. This creates a distraction for Yemo to attack the other Simerin. He's now in a struggle for the weapon. The Simerin that's now on his back fires his weapon at Yemo, but I kick his arm holding the weapon. Yemo moves out of the way, and the other Simerin gets hit. Yemo grabs the weapon and kills the other Simerin. Their bodies are burnt to a crisp. The air reeks of burning Simerin flesh.

"Grab his weapon," says Yemo. Without hesitation, I pick up the weapon from the black, burning Simerin flesh, and we flee into the woods.

A tree explodes right in front of me, and I have to shield my face from all the flying debris. Shots fire all around us. Intense heat flashes right behind my head, and the force knocks me onto the ground. Yemo pulls me up, and I'm back on my feet. More Simerin?

"That direction," Yemo yells as he turns and fires his weapon in the opposite direction. "Keep going! I'll catch up."

"I'm not leaving you!"

I see movement about fifteen yards away. I don't see Yemo, and I start to panic. I tell myself to stay calm, and I take a deep breath. I see the Monahdah from the alley. He found us, and he aims his weapon at Yemo. I press the glowing, white button with my thumb, and the crescent shape of the simerin weapon lets out a destructive blast of heat that shatters a large ponderosa. Yemo fires from his vantage point, but this Monahdah traitor has incredible speed, and he disappears into the trees.

There's a tug on my arm. "Over here," Yemo says pointing to a small clearing in the trees. I don't know what to look for. Although, I suppose I would know a spaceship if I saw one. "I don't see anything!" A beam of sunlight shines into the clearing. "Look closer." Like a mirage, a reflection of a spacecraft appears. Its surface reflects the trees like a mirror and blends right into the surroundings. Going into this flying machine scares the crap out of me, but that was before we were attacked. Yemo says something in Monahdah, and a door slides open.

"Secret password?"

"Voice activated."

We jump into the craft as more shots are fired from behind. The Monahdah traitor runs for the pod, but the hatch door closes on him in the knick of time.

Mother Earth Ship

When I first looked back at the Earth, standing on the moon, I cried.

—Alan Shepard 1971

Yemo says something to himself in Monahdah with a smile on his face. He's happy to be back in his pod. He enters symbols into a clear tablet, and we lift straight up into the atmosphere.

"Are you injured?"

"I don't think so." Cuts and scrapes cover my arms. It looks like I was dragged through glass.

A neon blue light flashes in a rhythmic pattern on a panel of different symbols. "What's that flashing light?"

"I'm contacting the nearest ship that we can board. These pods are only for short distances." He looks at my cuts, scrapes and bruises. "Are you sure you're okay?" Then he takes a hold of what used to be my braid. "It looks like you need a make over."

"What do you mean?"

"Your hair is..."

I reach back for my braid and there's only a little stub. "It's gone! It must look terrible." There're still very long locks in the front, but the back got fried.

"You can start a new trend in NeuMonah," he says attempting to lighten the mood.

I realize in this very moment that my brother has saved my life and risked his own doing so. I wouldn't be standing here right now if it weren't for him. The love I feel for him is stronger than I have ever felt. The feeling swells inside my heart and tears overflow. We hug.

"I love you, Yemo."

"I love you, Anah."

"You saved my life."

I look over his shoulder at the clear view of the Southwest directly out the round window. "My first trip to outer space."

"We're still in the atmosphere, about fifty miles above Earth."

"That means we're between the mesosphere and the thermosphere." This gives me goose bumps.

"I have something for those cuts and burns," he says opening a box containing first aid items.

My wounds heal as he rubs an ointment over them.

"A special ointment from NeuMonah?"

"It is special but not from NeuMonah."

"Another planet?"

"Yes. Aloe, from planet Earth." He grins, and we laugh hysterically. The aloe heals my wounds, and our laughter heals my soul.

A neon purple light flashes in unison with a neon blue light. "We've made contact with a ship," says Yemo. He studies a screen with symbols that I don't understand.

I look closely at the strange symbols. "What's all that?"

"They're sending me the location."

"How far away is the ship?"

Yemo points to a 3d map showing our destination. "It's close. 230,000 miles from our location is a worm hole. We enter the worm hole, and the station is on the other side."

"What? That's close?"

"Don't worry. Take a nap, and we'll be there before you know it."

Take a nap? I'm not a baby. Although, the adrenaline rush is quickly wearing off.

"There's not a whole lot to see between here and there that's interesting, unless, you think your moon is interesting. You'll get a close up view on the way." He nudges me and nods his head to the window. "This is the real prize. The best view for millions of miles."

I look out the window, and a tear rolls down my cheek at the remarkable view. We are now outside of the Earth's atmosphere. Mother Earth-ship floats like a blue marble in space, illuminated by the sun keeping everything living alive. I've seen pictures of Earth from space, but that doesn't prepare you for this! Everything from up here looks perfect, peaceful, and harmonious. It's hard to imagine evil and cruelty exist when experiencing tiny Earth from this perspective. I wonder about my existence and my role in life. I respect those who know their role, like my brother, Father and Victor, for those who are willing to die for that reason. Saving the planet from Simerin now seems even more consequential and our problems on Earth meaningless. For the second time since the night of the Halloween dance, I integrate with the infinite energy and become one with the mysterious force.

Floating Here In Space

"Anah, wake up. We're here."

"Victor?"

"No, it's me," says Yemo.

"Where's Victor? Where am I?" I'm disoriented and was in and out of lucid dreams.

"The way you feel is a common side effect from jumping. You're in my pod. We arrived at the station." He looks out the window. "See for yourself."

I can hardly believe what I see. "Holy!" There are other pods, hundreds, flying around like tiny ants next to this mother ship swarming with life.

He's pleased with my reaction. "Pretty cool, huh?"

It's beyond what I imagined. The main station is round. Slowly orbiting it, like moons, are three smaller stations. The entire conglomerate seems to be dependent on a nearby sun. "What is this place?"

"It's a station."

"How long has this been here?"

"I don't know. This is a newer location."

"There must be thousands of people!"

"Millions." Yemo gets in line with a row of pods, and we join in the flow of space traffic, leading us to a space town. "It's basically an artificial planet. It rotates around this sun and gets power and energy from it. Then an atmosphere is created. It can also disassemble quickly for departure."

"Is Victor here?" I say excitedly.

"Probably not."

"But he's out here somewhere… somewhere nearby, right?"

"Yes, but so are Simerin. Anah, remember there is a war going on."

Looking at this spectacle, one could easily forget.

Bouquet of Flowers

Everyone on board gives me an overwhelmingly warm welcome. Of course, I'm the only female monahdah, so feeling like a minority is an understatement. I take an extra-long shower. My room is comfortable and private. There's a bed with tan-colored silk sheets and a long, built-in shelf above the bed. Light shines on the walls from three amazing Mon stones given to me when we arrived. Each one is unique with a different geometric shape. I stand before a large window that has an incredible view of the space city and its activity. The color of the daytime sky, burnt orange, and the pods coming and going, remind me that I'm not home anymore. The orange atmosphere doesn't fill up the sky like the blue sky on Earth. Space can still be seen. So there's an eerie mixture of light and the darkness of space. What a strange dream this would be. A doorbell rings and jolts me back to reality, telling me this is all very real and really happening.

I quickly put on the clothes laid out for me of the softest, white fabric imaginable and open the door to a bouquet of flowers. Behind them stands the shortest Monahdah I've seen so far, a hair shorter than me.

"Oh, how sweet. Thank you, umm…"

"Lumi," he says revealing himself from behind the lily-like flowers. They're different shades of purple and pink with multiple layers of delicate, exotic petals.

"Thank you, Lumi. They're beautiful."

"I made them myself. They're a cross between a lily from earth and a flower from NeuMonah."

"What are they called?"

"If you don't mind, I want to call them Anah."

"I don't mind at all. I'm honored."

Lumi glows with pride. He bows deeply in response. That's when I realize the floor in front of the door is littered with flowers.

"When you feel up to a tour I will be delighted to show you around." He hands me the flowers.

"I look forward to it." He bows again and walks away.

It's strange being treated like royalty. Perhaps it's as strange for them to witness a female Monahdah. I look out my window again. Everything that has happened to me in the past year has led me up to this moment. The juxtaposition between now and then is overwhelming to think about. The unknown can be frightening and exciting at the same time. Knowing that I have the free will to make decisions and that I have a sense of power over my life makes me less fearful. However, until events unfold, what lies in the future will remain uncertain. Fleeing for my life was definitely an event I didn't expect to happen. I tell myself that I have the courage to face uncertainty. A year from now, I'll be on another planet. I'll meet my grandfathers and perhaps theirs as well. I don't know when I'll see my mother again, and I pray she'll know I'm okay. All I know right now is that I will return home as soon as I can and that seems dependent on this war with the Simerin.

There's another ring at the door. More flowers?

"Nahmah Anah," says a man with snow-white hair and magenta eyes. He gives me a single, but marvelous flower that shimmers whiter than white and is rimmed in magenta, the same color as his eyes.

"Nahmah."

He speaks in Monahdah, so I have to telepathically translate. He wants to fix my hair and has invited me to join him in his salon.

He turns and walks away, so I follow. Telepathic translation isn't perfect, so I hope he means now.

We walk in silence the rest of the way to a very white, sterile looking room. He gestures to a chair for me to sit in and starts to brush my hair or what's left of it. I look at myself in a mirror that reflects a 3D image of my head, and I can see the back of my head for the first time. It will take a miracle!

"What's your name?" He's not into small talk because he hasn't

tried to make conversation. Maybe it's the language barrier.

"Gio," he answers as he types something on a pad and walks out of the room.

While I sit and stare at myself in the 3D mirror, a machine lowers down from above, sucks my hair up and begins to cut my hair.

What the hell is this? "Gio?" I nervously call out.

He enters the room again. "Yes?"

"Ah…" I'm not sure what to say, but he answers. Roughly translated, he tells me to enjoy and relax.

The machine cuts my hair all around, simultaneously. Like a vacuum, it sucks my hair straight up. It forces air out like a big blow dryer. The machine finishes with a final blast of air and returns to the ceiling.

While I wait for Gio to return, I check out my new look in the mirror. The robot left it very layered and kept long pieces or strands in the front. No more braids or messy buns!

I'm pleasantly surprised by the results. "It's awesome!"

Gio doesn't show much emotion, but I sense satisfaction coming from him despite his lack of expression. "Thank you, Gio." He bows his head. People really like to bow around here. I guess it's a Monahdah thing.

I try to find my way back, but I've taken a wrong turn. A pair of alien creatures that have long noses like ant eaters walk by. I'm a little embarrassed because I'm lost. I guess it's a good time to ask Lumi for that tour.

"Sure," he answers right away.

"Although, I can't tell you where I am." I look around in every direction.

"Don't move. I'll be there in a jiffy."

I wonder why his English is so good. He must have spent time on earth.

"I watch your movies," he says from behind.

"Hi, Lumi," I say with relief.

"Nice. You look like one of those bad ass chicks out of a comic book."

"It's not too much, is it?"

"No, not at all. You look great."

He directs me down a path. "This is the wellness quarters. You've met Gio. He does hair, makeup, eye color, anything your heart desires." We turn a corner. "Here's where you can find material for that new outfit you have in mind."

"You mean I can design an outfit and have it custom made?" I think about Sophia and how excited that would make her.

"Of course, or choose something already made and have it altered."

"That's awesome."

Musical sounds come from a dark corridor. Lumi signals for me to follow him. We walk to a room where a small group of people play flutes, string instruments and metal disk drums that look like mini UFO's. "Here's where you can learn to play an instrument or meet with your band."

"Who are they?"

"They call themselves, DahmanKi."

"I think I know what that means, actually. It means guardian."

"Yes, Dahman means guardian and AmanKi means peace, so together it means, guardian of peace."

"You can see them perform tonight at Thule. I'd be happy to escort you there."

I think Lumi just asked me on a date. "What's Thule?"

"A place to chill, hang, or go a little crazy," he says with a smile.

I'm guessing the last movie he watched was from the eighties.

"Sure, why not?" I say, hoping he doesn't get the wrong idea.

"Anah, I know about you and Victor. Most of us here do."

"Really?"

"There's no such thing as a secret with us." He takes my hand and places it in the crook of his arm, leading me back down the hall.

"How long have you known?"

"Well, it was confirmed when you arrived, but there was a bit of a whisper going on for a while. Victor was here for part of his training before he left. It became obvious he was in love when he would communicate with you, so to speak." He gives me a wink.

"That hasn't happened in a while."

"Probably because MinnEnki told him to cut it out."

"My father? Well, that figures."

"Only because he felt it was putting you in jeopardy."

"Do you know if Victor is okay?"

"What does your heart tell you?"

"That he worries about me, all the time." I feel the truth in this for the first time.

"Then let him know you are fine."

My eyes swell up with tears. I hug Lumi with gratitude. "Thanks, Lumi."

"Anytime."

"What kind of training was he getting here?"

"What all Keepers do just before they head into battle," he says pointing to a room. "Come." I follow him down another dimly lit hall. Lumi instructs me not to speak, not even telepathically, before he enters into a room where someone sits with his legs crossed and eyes closed, chanting 'Om'. There are others in the room doing yoga. One Keeper has both legs behind his head, while another balances totally on his head without the use of his hands.

"An interesting way to prepare for battle," I say as we leave the room.

"They prepare in every way. Learning to master the mind and body is one. Well, that concludes this part of the tour. Perhaps we shall continue later? I could show you the gardens next time, my favorite part of the station."

"I would like that."

He escorts me the rest of the way to my room. I hug him and thank him again for his kindness.

"I'll come by later to escort you to Thule."

"I look forward to it."

Only Female on Board

I empty the contents of my backpack onto my bed. Since we left in such a hurry, I don't really have many belongings. And I left my phone behind at the coffee shop. Damn! I know I wouldn't be able to use it, but I regret not having it. Not to mention, that might be the one thing that will make Mom worry. I sit on the edge of my bed. I want to call my Mom so badly that it hurts. I wish I could have at least told her goodbye. I'm experiencing strong regret and have a lump in my throat. Everything has happened so fast.

I pull out a pair of jeans from my backpack. Underneath lies the Simerin weapon I took. It makes me uncomfortable, and I don't want to touch it. I saw what it can do. I need to find a safe place for it or give it to Yemo.

Where the hell *is* Yemo? This is the longest I've gone without him showing up, and I know I'm the only female on board.

Just then the bell rings. "Speak of the devil," I say as the door slides open.

"Miss me?" he asks.

"Just wondering where you've been."

He stares at me awhile, and I can tell he's trying to decide whether he likes my hair. "You don't like it?"

"I do. You just look older, less innocent. It took me a moment." He picks up the Simerin weapon.

"I don't want that in here. Can you take it?"

"You should keep it," he says handing me the weapon.

"You must be joking."

"Joking?" He puts the gun on the shelf. "I always mean what I say, Anah."

"Right. Anyway, I don't feel comfortable having it."

"You just need to know how to use it. You were awesome, you know."

"No, I don't."

"I think we make a good team. Maybe you should train."

"As a Keeper?" He must have temporarily lost his mind.

"It's in your blood."

"I don't think that's possible. Meirlies wouldn't risk it and neither would you, Yemo."

"If you want to train as a Keeper just say the word," he says with a grin.

I look at myself in the mirror. "So, what should I wear to Thule?"

"Whatever you want."

"Can't you offer some suggestions?"

"It's a party, lots of dancing. Hey, too bad you don't have the outfit you wore at your school the night we met."

"That was a Halloween costume." I roll my eyes. "That would be a little weird."

"You asked. Just wear what you have on."

"I'm gonna check out that clothing store." I give him a pleading look. "Come with me?"

"We don't have stores. But I'll come along."

The store, or whatever they call it, is filled with all kinds of fabric and ready-made outfits. I look around. "Is there someone to help?"

Yemo goes over and taps on a screen. "Go ahead. Say what you want."

"A new outfit," I say, feeling a little silly.

"What color?" it asks.

I look at Yemo for some ideas, but he's trying on a jacket. "I don't know."

"Here are some options." It actually shows pictures of ideas already in my mind.

"That's amazing!"

I make some adjustments in my mind, and so does the computer image. I'm seeing and creating my thoughts right before my eyes.

Afterwards, the computer instructs me to stand at the place where there's a glowing, blue light on the floor. A light follows the contours of my body, making perfect measurements. Less than ten minutes later, I collect my items from a window folded and ready to wear.

"Where is everyone, anyway? You'd never know there's millions of people in this space-city."

"Getting ready for tonight."

"You mean everyone will go to this thing?"

"It's a party and we love to party."

When we get back to my room, there are more flowers on the floor by the door. "They really need to stop with the flowers," I say picking them up. "I'm running out of room here."

While changing in the back room, there's a ring at the door, and I hear Yemo talking with Lumi.

"I'm almost ready," I announce, studying myself in the mirror wearing my new clothes. The dark gray fabric is form fitting and snug but at the same time light and comfortable. It actually doesn't feel like I'm wearing anything at all. My lace-up boots give the look the perfect finishing touch. My mind flashes back to the night at the club when I first met Victor. I was wearing my mother's leather jacket and the Mon ring I found in the pocket. I feel a ping of sadness that seems to linger over me like a shadow. My reflection shows how different I look with my new clothes and

my new hair, but it doesn't reflect how I've changed on the inside. It goes much deeper. So much has changed since I first met Victor.

"You look great, Anah," Yemo yells impatiently.

"You haven't even seen me yet." I walk out into the bedroom and wait for a response. "So... how do I look?"

"Amazing," says Lumi. *"Girl, you look incredible."*

"Thanks." I avert my eyes because he only wears a modest cover for his genitals. "And Lumi... you look...like you forgot to get dressed."

He laughs. "My outfit is seen when the lights go out." He dims the lights and slowly his whole body reveals tattoos in bright neon colors. His lips glow white, and his eyes are lined in the same matching shimmery white.

"Wow, glow in the dark tattoos. Is it permanent?"

"They last for a few days. They can change, too, depending on the light source."

I notice that Yemo is wearing a tie. "A tie? You hate ties."

"I think I like them now. This one's cool. It also glows. Check it out." The fabric glows intricate designs as he moves it around in the dim light.

"Shall we?" Lumi's glowing naked body leads the way.

We take a self-flying pod to the other side of the city and underneath a large glass dome. We walk up a ramp to the first level. A waterfall flows down the center. I look up at the height of the waterfall and see that there are multiple levels of the dome. Trees, exotic plants, and grass grow all around like a Japanese garden. Dreamy sounds of flutes, string instruments and metal drums fills the dome from above.

"Is that DahmanKi playing?" I say, recognizing the sound.

"Yes," says Lumi.

"Where are they?"

"We should go to the top," says Yemo.

We ride an open platform to the top level when I finally realize that this whole gathering was arranged in my honor. "Yemo, you should have warned me."

"Surprise!" he says.

The platform comes to the top. The music stops and all eyes are on me.

"Nahmah Anah," they greet me in unison. *"We are honored and delighted that you are now a part of this family. This congregation is in your honor, and may you have approval."*

I suddenly wish I could speak Monahdah, so I could respectfully reply. All eyes are on me as they wait for me to speak.

"I'm honored," I begin to stammer as I look into all the faces. *"I'm proud to be here and to be considered a part of this family. Nahmah."* I look up at Yemo, and he seems to approve.

We begin to mingle, and of course, more flowers come my way. *"When will it end?"* I ask myself. *"After everyone has given you one,"* says Yemo.

With each flower my heart is filled with a different sense of appreciation and admiration. Then I understand. They consider themselves a single entity. One living organism, like a beehive or an an aspen forest. Watching or waiting for many lifetimes, a few thousand years, and it has finally happened. It has bloomed.

Food and drinks are being served in a room that's behind the waterfall. I get myself a drink and observe this strange, unfamiliar crowd. Monahdah for the most part are very tall and fair. They range in skin tone, and some look almost albino with pale blue eyes. Unusual humanoid, insect beings are laughing in the corner with the long nosed aliens I had seen before. Then I notice humanoids with short child-like bodies with grayish skin tone, large eyes and very small ears—much like the little aliens that popular culture on Earth has made famous.

"Are they Monahdah?" I ask Yemo, looking at the little grays.

"They are not," he explains in Monahdah, and I'm pleased at how fast I'm catching on. *"They reside in space and don't live or settle organically on planets. Their work made this station possible. They're very docile, subservient aliens. As you can see, not every passenger here is Monahdah. We have peace treaties with them and*

other species. As a result, some live and work together on our stations."

A drum picks up a slow beat and dancing commences. Lumi's glowing body dances with another Monahdah. I follow Yemo to the edge of the balcony next to the waterfall and can make out figures dancing below. The drumbeat picks up its tempo and rhythm, summoning us to join in. The sound crescendos and soon everyone, including myself, moves entrancingly to a hypnotic tribal beat. The collective energy in the room captures me, and I've lost all sense of time, space, even reality. For a brief, cerebral moment, I notice everyone is wet with sweat and realize we've been dancing for a long time.

Lumi's spirit makes up for his size. He jumps over the balcony and splashes down below into the lake of the waterfall. His dance partner follows. Several people are now dancing and jumping into the water. My mind wanders to Victor and the memory of holding his hand as we jumped into the lake. I suddenly have an overwhelming feeling of guilt. He's somewhere putting his life on the line, and here I am dancing and enjoying myself like it's the last party on Earth, or in this case, the universe.

"I want to go back to my room," I tell Yemo.

"I know."

"I can find my way back."

"I'll check on you shortly then."

"I'm not a little kid, Yemo. I'll be fine. I really want to be alone right now."

"Let me know if you need anything."

I hug Yemo and thank him for the great celebration in Monahdah. *"Elohim davunsch. Lamu Nahmah."*

"MiLamu Nahmah." Says Yemo, as I turn and leave.

Never Paranoia, Only Perception

I haven't been to this part of the space-town. My sense of direction tells me I'm going the right way. I could take the pod back to my building but decide that the walk will do me some good. The street is completely empty since everyone is at Thule. The dead silence is unsettling after the sound and energy of the party. When I turn the corner, the distant sound of the drums dissipates. I have the strange sensation that someone is behind me, and I quickly turn around. No one is there, just an empty, dead, quiet walkway. Lights flicker on and off, and I tell myself to stay calm and that I'm perfectly safe. Although, wasn't a Monahdah not that long ago shooting at Yemo and I? There could be more than one loose cannon, right? I'm being paranoid. Victor told me, however, that there's never paranoia, only perception.

I turn down another walkway that looks familiar. It leads to a grand building with a dome roof. Moss, grass and other growing things cover the pathway that leads into the dome. My intrigue takes me further down the path and into a botanical garden. This must be the garden Lumi wanted to show me, however, when I reach an overlook, I see the garden becomes a forest that's at least a hundred acres. Trails lead to other trails meandering into hidden valleys with exotic trees with purple, puffball flowers, and plants from other worlds. I don't know my way around, and the orange sky is growing darker. As I cross over a creek bed, I decide not to stray beyond this point. A bird calls out a loud, startling, high-pitched trill to warn others that I'm trespassing. It echoes through the valley. My eyes adjust to the darkening, orange sky. The narrow trail disappears into a thick jungle of vegetation. The bird calls out a loud trill again. A shadowy figure twenty yards away crosses the narrow path in front of me. "Is someone there? Hello?" My voice carries across and echoes far away to an unknown location as if I'm in an echo chamber. The only reply comes from the flapping of wings in the tree above. The bird tires of my intrusion and flies away. I follow the bird's advice and retrace my steps back, leading me out of the forest.

After turning down three more pathways, I find my building and my room. I can't seem to shake this ill feeling. Maybe I should've had Yemo escort me, although I desperately needed the alone time. "Enter," I command the voice-activated door. It doesn't open. I'm pretty sure I have the right door. I'm reassured when I look down at the flowers on the floor. Yep, this is the right door. "Enter," I say loudly and clearly. This time the door slides open. Entering my room with sigh, I go to the back room where my bed is. The Simerin weapon still lies on the shelf above the bed where Yemo left it, even though I asked him to put it somewhere safe. I'm not sure why, but I put it under my pillow. I enter the bathroom and brush my teeth. When I spit into the sink, I hear movement coming from the front room and smell that very distinctive, unforgettable, nasty smell, which sets off every part of my 'fight or flight' response. I'm in danger. There's a presence in my room, and I need to act now. My heart rapidly beats. *"Yemo!"*

"Already on my way."

"Hurry!" A Simerin has trespassed into my room! Should I stay in the bathroom, or do I have a fighting chance if I go out? If I stay here, I'm cornered, so I leave the bathroom. He stands between me and the bed, and the weapon I put under the pillow. He looks at me but miraculously doesn't see me. He looks puzzled as he looks right through me! A skill I unwittingly used a few years ago in the band room when I accidentally walked in on my teachers! I could sneak around him and go for the weapon, or I could get the hell out of the room.

The instant I make a run for it, he senses my movement and attacks. He gets ahold of my clothing, but I break free, ripping the fabric of my top. I fly out the door and run down the hall. He's right behind me. I'm approaching the corner of the hall, so I'll have to slow down to make the turn or else crash directly into the wall. If I slow down, he'll be able to grab me. I decide to go as fast as I can straight for the wall. I'll jump. I accelerate to my top speed. Just before I smash into the wall, I close my eyes. I have the sensation that I can't breathe, like I'm underwater. The sensation lasts longer than my previous experience with Yemo in the car. I'm dead. Oh my God! Am I dead? If I didn't exist, would I be thinking about it? I lose track of who I am, my body, my mind and what I'm doing. POP! I hear it loudly, and I crash right into someone. I look up at a very tall, exceptionally good-looking guy. He has thick, caramel-colored hair and a solid build with pale aquamarine eyes.

"Excuse me," he says in a loud room full of people dancing to a live band.

Where the hell am I? I look around and see two familiar people dancing and having fun. I know those people. Who are they? Where am I? Oh, that's right, I'm at the club. It's coming back to me. I look back up at the guy I bumped into.

"Sorry," I say, feeling terribly disoriented. I'm suddenly not feeling well and go to the bathroom. "What the hell is happening?" I feel like I'm having some serious déjà vu. Do I know that guy I just banged into? I'm sure I do. He didn't know me, though. I splash water on my face and look at myself in the mirror. What has happened to my hair? It's short, and I have no memory of cutting it!

"I think I like it better long," says a voice.

I spin around. "Who the hell are you?" I ask some strangely familiar guy who has just trespassed into the girls' bathroom.

"Anah, we need to go, like now." He steps closer to me.

"How the hell do you know my name?"

"Anah, you've jumped too far. You're experiencing memory loss. You're not going to believe me, but I'm your twin brother. Our father is from another planet. That hunk you bumped into out there is your boyfriend. We were on a space station... that's right, in outer space. We were partying, dancing, having fun, but you decided to go back to your room alone when you were attacked by a Simerin."

My head is spinning. "I'm going to scream for help at the count of three if you don't leave."

"That guy out there that you bumped into is your boyfriend, remember?"

"One."

"Victor. You remember him."

"Two."

"Oh and Sophia..."

"What do you know about Sophia?"

"She's your best friend, and we hooked up after I met her at Thanksgiving."

"Where's my ring? I had a ring, I think," remembering a piece of a puzzle.

"Yes, that's right, you did, you will," stammers Yemo.

"If he's my boyfriend, then why didn't he know me?"

"I think because this is where you first met."

"Victor? That's his name?"

"Yes?" Victor answers back.

"Holy shit, he just answered me."

Someone is opening the door to the bathroom. Yemo grabs my arm and drags me into the bathroom stall. "What the hell are you doing?"

"We're hiding."

"From who?"

"Shhh," Yemo puts his finger to my mouth, "from you."

I sneak a peak over the bathroom stall, and there I am looking down at the Mon ring on my finger.

Holy shit. I crouch back down behind the door. Yemo signals me to be still, and we quietly wait for me to leave the bathroom. This whole experience is surreal, especially listening to me in the adjacent stall. Like slowly remembering a dream several hours after waking up, more pieces come together.

"I was attacked?" I ask him in my head.

"Yes, and you jumped to escape. I managed to jump on board at the last second, and I'm here to bring you back. You jumped so far, I was turned around and disoriented until I saw you bump into Victor."

"If I could, why would I go back to a place where I was in danger?"

"I killed the Simerin that attacked you."

I put my had over my mouth so I don't say anything out loud. "Holy shit, this is for real?"

"Yes, and we need to leave here. We've already been here too long."

"I want to see Victor first."

He firmly grabs ahold of my hand. "We need to go now, and we need to leave without anyone seeing you."

He peeks out the door, and the sound of the music fills the bathroom. "Ready?"

"Wait." I grab the keys I left hanging on the bathroom door hook. "I just want to see him before I go." I quickly scan the room.

"Hurry. Don't let him see you."

He's staring right at me, not this me, but the other me. I want to run to him, but Yemo has a strong hold on my hand in case I do something stupid. Just before I turn away, Victor gives me his smile from the side of his mouth, and my heart explodes.

I find someone to give my keys to. "Someone left these keys in the bathroom. They belong to Anah, she drives a white Toyota…."

Before I can finish, Yemo drags me through the dancing crowd, and we're out through the main doors into the cool night air. He's running fast and dragging me along with him. I try to keep up.

"Ready?" he says in my head, and then it happens. We jump. Everything is dark, and I lose all sense of time and space. Am I dead? No, this is what happened before. I hear the loud pop, like someone just stuck a pin into a balloon. I open my eyes and try to refocus. I'm lying on a floor. Yemo still holds my hand very tightly.

Victor Knows the Way

Yemo looks disoriented. *"Where are we?"* Light flickers on and off, then back on again.

"Yemo, are you okay? What's wrong?"

"I'm experiencing memory loss. What just happened?"

"We were dancing at Thule, and I went back to the room and was attacked by a Simerin, and you came to rescue me right before I jumped too far into the past when I first met…" I don't finish my sentence. I saw Victor, and I want nothing more than to be with him. "We must be back at the station."

"Something doesn't feel right," he says looking around trying to orient himself.

"You lost your memory. I felt disoriented at first, too. It will pass."

"What I mean is, despite the disorientation, I sense we are trespassing. Don't you sense something?"

"No..." I sniff the air, "but I do smell something." I put my hand to my nose in disgust. "I've smelled it before. When Simerin attacked us in the woods and when one was in my room." A flash of panic washes over me. "Holy shit, we're on a Simerin ship. We're dead. I'm so sorry, Yemo, for getting you into this."

"Don't panic just yet. You brought us here, so there must be a reason."

"Like what?"

"What were you thinking before we jumped?"

"I don't remember."

"Were you thinking about Simerin?"

"I don't know."

"What was your first thought when we came here?"

Someone comes down the hall. We quickly get up and turn a corner to hide. Yemo sneaks a peak around the corner. A Simerin enters a dark corridor and disappears into a room.

"Try to focus, Anah," he says impatiently.

"I'm trying. It's hard to think when you're scared shitless."

"Of course! You were thinking of Victor."

"Yeah, probably, but why would that bring us here?"

Just then we hear someone cry out in pain as if he's being tortured.

"I think we just got our answer," says Yemo. "He might be a prisoner in that room."

My blood runs cold. "What are they doing to him?"

"They're doing it to get to you, Anah. It's a trap," says Yemo.

"You mean that's really not him in there crying out in pain?" I'm about to lose it.

"Whether it is or not, the fact remains that it's to trap you."

"No, not this time. They don't know we're here. They're trying to get information from him as to my whereabouts. Victor fell into one of *their* traps. And we're going to get him the hell out!"

"Don't communicate with him. The Simerin will detect something."

"Then you must, so he can prepare an attack."

My heart is pounding fast. My body knows what it's about to do, and my hands begin to shake. "What's the plan?"

"We wait for that Simerin to leave before we go in. We'll try to do it without setting off any alarms."

"There could be more than one in there, though."

"I'm pretty sure there's only one."

"What if there's not, then what?"

"Then we have to kill him."

The Simerin leaves the room and turns down the hallway.

"Let's do this," says Yemo.

"Wait! How do we get out? I don't think I can jump again."

"Victor knows the way," says Yemo.

"How do you know?"

With a grin he says, "He just told me."

A tear runs down my cheek. Victor's in there, and we're about to save him! We run down the dark corridor and enter the doorway.

Oh my God! Victor's naked, and restrained. His body has burn marks and cuts on his chest where they've tortured him. He's pinned to a wall, held by some kind of invisible force.

"Remember. Don't talk to him. Don't touch him. Nothing," Yemo instructs.

"The panel behind you," says Victor. *"We don't have much time."*

My hands tremble as I locate and press one of the two buttons on the panel. Victor's arms and legs are set free. His body falls to the floor. It takes all I have to not run to him and hold him. Yemo helps Victor along the way as he gives us directions to the landing dock. The place is crawling with Simerin.

"There's my fighter," Victor says pointing.

"We'll never make it," I say.

Victor stares at me, unable to control his smile. My eyes swell up with tears of joy, and I know nothing will ever rival this moment, that is, if we survive.

The Simerin suddenly look agitated. They all begin to scurry around, and they're actually leaving.

"They've just discovered that I've escaped," says Victor.

"Good timing. Now we have a chance," says Yemo.

We make a break for the fighter. Victor says something in Monahdah, and the hatch to the fighter opens. He gives a few more commands, and the engine starts. As we exit the landing dock, he shoots all the Simerin fighters. They explode one by one.

"Sweet!" Yemo yells out in excitement.

"Sweet?" says Victor.

"That's his new earth lingo," I say.

Victor looks at me again and gives me a smile.

"Is it okay to talk to him now?"

"I guess," Yemo says jokingly, with a renewed sense of humor.

I don't know what to say first. He puts his hands on my face, and our foreheads touch.

"I like your hair," he says breaking the silence.

"I had to cut it." I hold back tears.

We embrace, and I smell his scent and melt right into his arms.

"You saved me, Anah."

Yemo clears his throat. "*We* saved you."

"Being that it's my fault, it's the least I could do," I say, overcome with guilt, looking at his scars and wounds.

"Sorry to interrupt you love birds, but it looks like someone's crashing the party."

There's a sudden jolt, and I lose my balance. A Simerin is right on our tail.

"It's okay. Nothing was damaged," says Victor, looking at his controls. *"Shield's still on."*

Yemo fires away using the controls in the back of the cockpit, but the Simerin maneuvers well and avoids every strike.

This could be the end. I rescued Victor just so we could die together in this fighter.

"I've made contact with our ship. We're not far," says Victor.

"We got another one. We have two on us," says Yemo, in Monahdah.

"Alrighty then," says Victor. He stops on a dime, and they fly right by.

Another fighter appears on the other side of the Simerin fighters. "It's AmanKi," says Yemo. Victor's father arrives just in time to provide back up, and we all share a flicker of hope. AmanKi and Victor fire away at the Simerin fighters trapped in the middle. One after the other, the fighters explode.

"Now *that's* sweet!" Victor says.

Victor's father escorts them all the way back to the dock.

Vunsch

Victor lands the fighter on the dock, and the first person we see waiting for our safe arrival is Father. His somber demeanor doesn't fool me. His fear and his relief that we've made it back, and also his frustration with Victor, is palpable. It's a good assumption that Victor hasn't followed Father's orders.

We exit the craft and embrace. His body trembles. "Meirlies, we're fine. It's okay."

"Come. We need to talk," he says throwing Victor a pair of pants. "All of you, follow me." Like school children, we march behind. A door opens to an empty room. The mood is heavy, and it feel like we're about to get reprimanded. Victor looks pale and weak. What he really needs is some medical attention.

"Meirlies, Victor needs a doctor. Don't you think he's been punished enough?" Victor and Yemo give me a surprised look. I guess only I can get away with talking to him in such a way.

"Yes, and yes. Victor is an excellent Keeper but young and brash."

"This is my fault," I say, catching my breath so I don't cry.

"Nothing is anyone's fault except for Simerin and that Monahdah traitor."

The door slides open again, and AmanKi walks in. I'm actually glad to see him. He stares at Victor and his surface wounds, which are already showing signs of healing. AmanKi stands before me and kneels. He takes my hand and places it on his heart and allows me to feel his gratitude beyond what words can express. He is also grateful for my safe return.

"Victor would have done the same for me. In fact, that's what he thought he was doing. Simerin could have killed me twice now. I don't know what they want with me."

"You're worth more to them alive than dead," says Meirlies. "They want you as leverage."

"Well, that's a relief. I was beginning to wonder if they wanted to… to mate with me."

"They can't," says Meirlies. "They change their sex in order to breed, bsut since they started cloning, their natural way of breeding rarely happens."

I think about how unattractive they are and how they smell like rotting trash. "Weird, however, not unheard of. Slugs and some fish can change their sex in order to breed," I say, bewildered.

"Anah would not have survived if it wasn't for Victor training her. She's alive because of him, not because of me," Yemo says hanging his head down. Yemo sits back heavily into his chair. "My apologies, Meirlies, that the New Mexico drohan escaped."

Wow. This is unexpected. My brother is more humble than I thought.

"I'm proud of you, Yemo, more than you'll ever know," Father says placing his hand on Yemo's shoulder. "Vunsch!"

Victor puts his hand on Yemo's other shoulder and says it too, "Vunsch."

This is a big moment for my brother who never felt worthy before Meirlies until now. "What does Vunsch mean in this context?" I ask.

"It's like saying, 'Good job' or 'Congratulations,'" says Victor.

I look at my brother with the respect he deserves. "Vunsch."

Naked On A Table

Victor's chest slowly rises and falls with his breath. He lies naked on a giant slab of Mon stone in the recovery room. The table has a soft, gel-like surface that molds to the muscular curvature of his body. This is the first time I've actually seen him sleep. Victor has four broken ribs and a fractured jawbone. Dressed with aloe and honey, his burn wounds on his chest and abdominals are almost healed. His physical strength gradually heals. He shows some signs of post traumatic stress as his body twitches with the memory of pain. This warns me of how vulnerable he is, of his mortality. He can easily die. There's no super-hero powers here. I put my hand on top of his. Seeing him in this condition because of me makes me angry. He thought he was rescuing me but fell into a Simerin's trap and nearly lost his life.

The ship we're on isn't as nice as the station we were on before I jumped to escape. It serves its purpose as a battle station but lacks in comfort and leisure. There aren't any large gardens or places to get your hair styled or parties like at Thule. What should I do now? I don't feel safe anywhere, but being on the same ship as my father, brother and boyfriend gives me some feeling of security. Meirlies hasn't agreed yet, but I've made a request to stay on this ship. Victor is here, and that's what matters.

"He'll be stronger than before," Meirlies says as he enters the room. He puts a reassuring hand on my shoulder. *"I'll let you stay on the ship for the time being. When I tell you to go to NeuMonah, however, you must go."* He stares at me with his glowing, hazel eyes that are strong yet sincere. I have to remind myself that these are the eyes of my father. *"I'm proud of you too, you know,"* he says as he turns to leave the room.

"Meirlies, *If they take me, if the Simerin capture me, don't give into them."*

He stares at me long and hard. *"I won't let that happen."*

"But if it does…you can't let them win…even if it means not saving me."

"Their tactics are for one end only, to gain control Earth and this sector. If they don't capture you they will try to find another way. Either way we will stop them." He looks down at the floor with a heavy heart. "Sometimes a few must be sacrificed to secure the future."

"We're not talking about a few. We're talking about the whole planet. I wouldn't be able to live with that. Earth is my home, you know."

"I don't mean to sound cold, but planets come and planets go. This is something young Earth will someday face, whether in a galactic war or general collapse."

"You wouldn't say the same thing if we were talking about NeuMonah, would you?"

"I understand your attachment to Earth. This planet means more to us than you think. We have fought and died for this planet before, and we'll continue to do so."

"Then you understand what I'm trying to say. I'm willing to die for my planet."

"Your father will not let you die in the hands of Simerin," interrupts Victor's voice, "And we won't give in to them." Victor slowly sits up on the edge of the platform.

"You shouldn't get up. You need to rest," I say.

"Who can rest with you two in here?"

"I'm sorry. We'll leave."

"It's okay." He says taking my hand. "I'm tired of resting."

"You should get rest as well, Anah," Meirlies says as he turns to leave. He stops before exiting. *"I admire your strength and courage."*

Victor slides his legs into white, silky pants. That's when I realize I'm wearing the same clothes that I wore to Thule, except now they're torn.

"You are as stubborn as your father," says Victor.

"Is that a Monahdah trait?"

"Stubbornness and compassion, sometimes they go hand in hand." He tucks a long strand of hair behind my ear and leans in for a kiss.

It's been over a year since we've been physically intimate, and my body trembles from his touch. While we kiss, he lifts me onto the Mon table, and our bodies entwine. The Mon stone returns to me vital energy depleted from being in a survival state of mind and from the jumps.

Victor interlaces his fingers with mine. "I love you," he says for the first time in English. Before I reply, a red flashing light comes on accompanied by a loud alarm.

"What the hell's that?" I ask.

Victor gets off the table. "Everyone's being called to the landing dock."

"Is this normal?"

"No."

"I'm coming with you."

"You should stay here."

"I don't think so."

Someone running down the hall collides with us as we step out of the room. There's a jolt and a loud explosion. We slam into the wall and then fall onto the floor.

"What's going on?"

"We must be under attack." Victor gets back on his feet. "Hurry!"

We make it to the landing dock, and there's lots of confusion. I'm not sure what to do or where to go. Yemo runs in our direction. "Anah, you're coming with me." He turns to Victor. "Simerin got past our ships. They're taking over the planet, and you're part of the rescue mission."

"I'm going then, too!"

There's another explosion, and everyone falls to the floor.

My father helps me up. "Go with Yemo, Anah."

"I'm not leaving Victor!"

Yemo grabs ahold of my arm. "We need to leave while we still can."

I look at Victor, and he takes my hand. "You must go, Anah!"

"The ship's shields are malfunctioning. I think they hacked in. You really have no time!" my father says urgently.

"What about Mom?"

"We'll do what we can."

I run in the opposite direction from Victor. I pause to look back. Several fighters explode from Simerin fire as soon as they exit the landing dock. *"They're not making it out!"*

"Victor will," Yemo says confidently.

We retreat to a ship that's connected to the main hall. Like a giant puzzle piece it begins to separate by the main ship. There's an incredible explosion, and we're thrown across the floor by the blast.

"We're okay," says Yemo staggering to his feet, but we both know something is terribly wrong. We look out a window and only see fire and debris throughout space. The main battle station has been destroyed.

"Holy shit, that was a close one!" The pilot with a strangely familiar accent says.

I sit down and try to recover. "What just happened?"

"They hacked into the system, and shut down our shields," says the pilot. "When we separated from the main ship I was able to get the shield working again, and not a second too late."

Yemo gestures to the pilot. "This is Paki. He's not Monahdah."

"Nope," he laughs, "one hundred percent Jamaican."

"How, may I ask, did you… ?"

"How did I end up with these guys?" He laughs again. "I was abducted by aliens." He chuckles. "Only joking. I was adopted. It wasn't against my will, I don't think."

He makes me smile. It's refreshing to be around someone with a positive attitude and a sense of humor. "It's nice to meet you, Paki." I offer my hand and see that I'm trembling.

"It's an honor to meet you, and a miracle. Now just make yourself comfortable, and enjoy the ride."

"That won't be possible until I know they're alive."

Then I hear Victor's voice. *"Anah? Are you there?"*

"I'm here! You're okay?"

"We're all here."

Yemo and I hug with relief.

Training

Yemo flips me onto my back for the third time, and this time I get the wind knocked out of me. We're in the Kalari, the room where we practice hand-to-hand combat. He says I'm not ready for sword-and-shield combat yet, which he has just proven again by taking me down. It's not plausible, anyway, that I'll be walking around with a sword and shield if I'm attacked. It just looks really cool, and I look forward to trying it out. We practice different fighting positions that I named after animals, so I can distinguish them. Lion pose is used mostly to confront your opponent.

During the first four months on the ship worrying about Victor, my father and Mother and all of Earth, I felt emotionally impaired and helpless. I didn't feel the need to get out of bed or eat. Blindsided by depression, I didn't see it coming. I slowly drowned and was unable to swim to the surface. Yemo, once again, rescued me. He reached down and pulled me up. Now, I feel like I can breathe again. He put me on a special diet to boost my energy and mood. We don't get any other natural source of energy in space such as sunlight, and there aren't any Mons on board.

He's been harder on me than what I expected from this training. He overcompensates because he doesn't want me to be treated differently since I'm a girl, and his sister.

Lying on my back, I say, "I'm done. I need a break."

Paki gives me his hand. "He's way too hard on you, Anah."

"He thinks I should be trained like he was. Like any Keeper."

"I'm doing it for your own good," says Yemo. "You would be dead if those Simerin wanted you dead!"

"But she's not!" says Paki. "She's here getting killed by you!"

"Don't you have a ship to fly?" Yemo pulls his long grown-out locks of hair away from his face. That's when I notice new lines on his forehead. He has taken on more stress than he should at his age, and I feel partly responsible.

"It's okay, Paki. I don't mind. My brother is making up for lost time," I say, and I wipe the sweat from my neck. "He needs your magic feet," I say, hoping he hears the overture to his amazing massage.

"That's why I'm here," says Paki.

"Oh... then why didn't you say so?" Yemo says, putting his arm around Paki.

We follow Paki to a dimly lit room with candles burning. The room is infused with the smell of hot oils. In the center of the room hang two knotted ropes. Paki points to the mat lying underneath the ropes. "Ladies first," he says.

I remove most of my clothes and lie face down on the mat. After applying hot oil on my back, arms and legs, Paki holds the rope to balance himself and firmly uses his feet to massage my body. "Is that too much pressure?"

"It hurts, but I'm fine. I'm just really stiff today," I manage to say as Paki glides his feet down my back.

"Not when I'm done with you," he says.

After my massage, I enjoy a hot steam bath allowing the oils to soak in. Yemo comes in after his massage.

"Paki is right. I'm too hard on you. I shouldn't expect you to be a fighter overnight. And I shouldn't take out my frustration on you while teaching you to fight." The truth comes out now that his tension has been pressed out by Paki's feet.

"It's okay. No need to apologize. It must be hard for you not to be there, in the fight with them. To do what you're trained to do." I use my towel to wipe the sweat dripping down my face from the steam.

"There's no other place I'd rather be than here," he says.

"What is this fighting called, what you're teaching me?"

"It's a combination of things. Some of the skills are ancient forms of fighting and self defense. You need to be very flexible— not so much strength but agility."

"That explains all the yoga-like moves."

"It could get you out of a tight bind. Like the one you experienced with the Simerin in the woods. He had you pinned down. Now you would be able to escape that situation."

"I remember all your moves against that Simerin. It was incredible."

"There's a similar skill on Earth. They call it Kalaripayattu. When you learn these skills, you will be empowered."

I meet Yemo at the Kalari every day after my morning routine of strengthening with weights, stretching exercises, and a juice break. I'm excited by my progress. I can finally extend my leg up the wall in a standing split. This is important for high kicks. I enter the Kalari with hopeful anticipation. I'm ready for the sword and shield, but Yemo hands me a big, blue scarf. The scarf drapes across my arm and hangs down to the floor. "What's this?"

"It's your weapon."

"You've become quite the comedian."

"You think I'm joking again?"

Yemo whips around me and has the scarf wrapped around my arms and neck, and I'm pinned down on the floor. "Okay, okay. Jeez... untie me already!"

"When you're caught off guard, you can use a scarf to defend yourself."

"I see that. Now will you unravel me?"

Yemo shows me several moves with the scarf, and it's surprisingly effective. He wraps the scarf around my arms, neck, then behind my back. I'm face down on the floor and completely immobile.

"Now you try," he says as he picks up the sword. He lunges toward me with the sword. I quickly wrap the scarf around his arm and disarm him.

Several months pass, and I perfect the moves with the scarf, and even invent a few moves of my own. "Really good, Anah. That's when you know you've mastered a skill. You use it intuitively, and it becomes an extension of who you are in every way."

After each training, we're rewarded with a massage from Paki's magic feet to prevent our muscles from tightening up, which is especially welcoming since we've been without our precious Mon. Paki slides his foot up and down my back. I reflect on how I've lost track of time since I've started my training. The time spent in the Kalari has passed to my benefit. I haven't lost my mind thinking about Mom, Victor, my father, and their mission to save Earth. Are they dead or alive? I don't know, and it's been a year since we departed on the ship before the explosion.

"I want you to be the first to know," Paki begins, interrupting my thoughts, "before I make the announcement to everyone, because I appreciate your patience, and you resisted the temptation to nag me, and to read my mind, and—"

"Just say it, Paki, before I do read your mind."

"We are on course for only three more days, or seventy more hours, to be exact, to be on the beautiful, emerald shores of NeuMonah."

I can't believe my ears! I gave up asking because he would scold me like a child, telling me that water will boil faster if you look the other way. Since I learned to put all my focus into my training, I was able to forget about our journey and sleep soundly at night as soon as my head hit the pillow. "This is incredible news! I can't tell you how happy this makes me!" I'm too excited to finish my massage. I spring up, hug Paki, skip the steam bath and head straight for the showers.

After showering, I catch a glimpse of myself in the mirror. I started my training about eight months ago. I look at the unfamiliar image in the mirror. It's not because of a new haircut or new clothes this time that make me look different. I hardly recognize my physique. There's little body fat, and I have defined muscles. I can label each one; abdominal muscles, biceps, triceps. What's most interesting is that my mind feels sharp and clear, and my body can work for my mind. I have a new sense of confidence and control. I smile internally at my transformation.

Underwater World

I stare out the window at my new home and refuge. After our year-long journey, seeing an actual planet occupy space is reassuring yet very surreal. I imagine this is what early explorers on earth experienced when they finally see land after many months out at sea. Adjusting to the bright light reflecting off the waters, I have to squint to look out over the horizon. Only water and the shadows of pods transporting the crew members from the ship dance across the glassy surface. "Where do we land?"

"We don't exactly land," Paki answers.

The pod dives into the water and becomes a submarine. We travel for several hours through ocean valleys, canyons and dark tunnels. We pass through a magical, underwater world with beautiful, strange sea creatures, and a maze of glowing magenta plants that come up out of the dark depths of the water in search for light, blooming a pure white, multi-petaled flower that attracts birds to its sweet fragrant nectar. We carefully maneuver through a city of neon, coral towers that grow several hundred feet tall. As we climb up to the surface, a school of dolphin-like mammals playfully follow us. They're white with blue stripes on their backs, and they have large flippers that allow them to propel themselves into the air when they jump out of the water. They control their webbed dorsal fin to go up or down. Pretty cool!

We travel through a kind of canal, and finally we arrive at marina. My heart beats with anticipation as Paki brings our pod up next to a hundred other pods docked at this port.

Yemo turns to me and offers his hand. "Are you ready?"

I wrap my new weapon around my head and neck and take my brother's hand. I don't know what I should be ready for; I guess everything and anything. Like meeting my new family and friends or simply breathing the air and walking on the soil of a completely different planet that has been home to my fathers for thousands of years. This is my new home, and this is not a dream.

Light floods into the pod as the hatch opens. I look at my brother fondly. "Lamu Nahma."

"MiLamu Nahma."

The End of Part 1

Vocabulary

Mon — Rock/planet. In the context of the story, it's a special stone from planet Mon that has cosmic energy.

Monahdah — A person from the planet Mon. Mon was taken by the Simerin in a war.

Simerin — Enemy alien race of the Monahdah.

NeuMonah — Name of a utopian planet colonized by the Monahdah.

Anah — Sister/female brother

Mahna — Brother

Meirlies — Father

Minniedah — My son

Nahanah — Goddess

Adamah — Human

Drohan — Traitor

Nahmah — I love you/hello/greetings

PrimmonKi — Female (from Earth.).

Lamu Nahma — Thank you/I graciously accept

MiLamu Nahma — You're welcome/I graciously give

Ki — Earth

AmanKi — Peace. Also the name of Victor's father.

Dahrman — Guardian

DahrmanKi — Guardian of peace/Name of the band.

Vunsch — Wonderful/congratulations

Elohim — Celebration

(Da)vunsch — (Was)wonderful

Elohim davunsch — The celebration was wonderful.

Da — Is/was/here

MinnEnKi — Earth Lord. Name of Anah's father.

ShanahMi — Forgive me or I'm at fault.

Nos — We shall

SzusahDah — Unite

Ma — And

Florah — Prosper/flourish/bloom

39821902R00168

Made in the USA
Middletown, DE
23 March 2019